1

'Lucy Mary O'Malley, you must be clean daft!' Aunt Harriet had exclaimed.

The accusation was one of Aunt Harriet's favourites, employed whenever her niece took it into her head to do something particularly outrageous. In Aunt Harriet's eyes anything that deviated in the smallest degree from the strictly conventional was termed outrageous, and Lucy sometimes felt as if she had lived every second of her eighteen years in an atmosphere of tongue clicking disapproval.

It was the harder to bear because Lucy was actually very fond of her precise, fussy aunt and wished she could conform to the ideal of a gentle, dutiful niece instead of having her red head stuffed full of romantic fancies and eyes that blazed green fire when her temper was roused!

'It's the Irish in you,' Aunt Harriet said sadly. 'Your poor father had it too.'

Lucy could just remember the small

red-haired man with the soft brogue and the long fingers who had brought her to Aunt Harriet's house.

'For where else could I leave my poor motherless darling than with her own mother's elder sister!' he had demanded rhetorically. 'Sure, I'll be sending for her as soon as I'm settled. You'll not be the loser by taking her in or my name isn't Patrick Lucius O'Malley!'

'And it certainly cannot have been,' Aunt Harriet said dryly, 'because we've not seen hair nor hide of him from that day to this!'

She had taken in her small niece out of duty and, because she was basically a kind-hearted woman, had done her best for the child. Harriet Peabody's best consisted of rearing Lucy to be as much a lady as limited financial means would permit.

'True gentility is bred in the bone and has nothing to do with one's income,' she was fond of saying.

Her own income, like her house, was tiny. She had done wonders with her limited resources, feeding and clothing her niece and paying for her to attend the local high school where the more affluent children of the district went. Lucy was bright at her lessons and Aunt Harriet had hoped to launch her as a schoolteacher or even as a governess into one of the big manufacturer's families, but Lucy had left school at sixteen and gone off to Sawyer's Mill to obtain a job as a clerk.

'A most unfeminine occupation! I never wanted a niece of mine to go into the mill,' she had lamented.

'I'm not really in the mill,' Lucy had tried to explain. 'I'm in the counting office with my own desk.'

From the office with its glass partition she could look down into the main shed where the looms clattered deafeningly all day long and the girls paddled about in water up to their ankles because the raw cotton had to be kept moist lest it dry and snap. The air in the shed was filled with minute specks of cotton and most of the older workers had bad chests as a consequence of breathing in the fibres, but up in the counting office the air was relatively clear and the clatter of the looms muted.

Aunt Harriet had stifled her objections and even contrived to boast a little to her neighbours.

'Oh, Lucy is very highly regarded in her

employment! She is very quick at figures, you know, and very neat. A young lady gives a certain tone to a business, I always say.'

There was every indication, she had considered, that Lucy was settling down. With her rebellious mane confined into a heavy plait and her trim figure encased in high-necked white blouse and ankle-length serge skirt, she looked as ladylike as even Aunt Harriet could wish. Only the long, green eyes, raised briefly from the ledgers, glinted rebellion.

But nobody could have been adequately prepared for her calm announcement made at the supper-table on that chill January evening, and Aunt Harriet's initial reaction had been one of complete stupefaction. She had blinked at her niece and said, faintly,

'You're going to—what?'

'I'm going to China,' Lucy repeated calmly.

'To—I'm not sure I heard you correctly, dear. I could have sworn you said you were going to China.'

'I did say it. Surely you've heard of China, aunt.'

'Of course I've heard of it,' Aunt Harriet

said, a little nettled. 'Everybody has heard of it, but people don't actually go there.'

'Missionaries do.'

'Oh, *missionaries!*' Aunt Harriet dismissed them with a flick of her hand.

'And diplomats go there and businessmen and merchants. Hundreds of people go to China,' Lucy said recklessly.

'Are you thinking of training for the Missions?' Aunt Harriet asked, peering at her niece. Lucy had never shown any sign of being particularly religious, but one never knew how these things might take a young girl.

'Goodness, no!' Lucy said, looking amused. 'I can't see me converting the heathen.'

Aunt Harriet couldn't see it either, but she was far from being reassured.

'I'm going to be married,' Lucy said, and poured herself another cup of tea.

Aunt Harriet closed her eyes briefly. She had always hoped, of course, that dear Lucy would eventually enter the matrimonial state, but she had an uneasy feeling that her notion of a respectable alliance was not what her niece had in mind.

'To a Chinese gentleman. I am going to

be married to a Chinese gentleman,' Lucy was saying.

'But we don't know any Chinese people,' Aunt Harriet said blankly.

'There was a party of them came to the mill this morning,' Lucy said. 'A trade delegation, touring Lancashire to study working conditions in the cotton industry. Mr Sawyer himself brought them round, and afterwards he told me that one of them had offered for my hand on his son's behalf, and he asked me if I would accept and I said that I would.'

It was then that Aunt Harriet had pushed back her chair and risen, exclaiming, 'Lucy Mary O'Malley, you must be clean daft!'

'Arranged marriages are quite common in China,' Lucy argued.

'But not in Oldham,' Aunt Harriet said flatly. 'And how can you be sure it's marriage they were talking about? Why, I've heard tales about innocent young girls being lured into the slave markets of the east.'

'Prince Chang Lee is not a white slaver!' Lucy exclaimed, laughing.

'A prince?' Aunt Harriet sat down again with a slight bump. 'Are you trying to tell me that this man is a prince?'

'Prince Chang Lee,' Lucy nodded. 'His father is a mandarin. He was with the trade delegation—the father, not the son. I've not met the son yet.'

'My dear, you cannot possibly marry a man you've never even met,' Aunt Harriet said. 'I'm sorry, but that is positively my last word on the subject.'

It was not of course. She had a great many more words to pour out in the days that followed, and in that lay her greatest mistake. If she had kept silent Lucy might have seen for herself that her course of action was completely impractical, but she brought forward so many objections that the girl felt honour-bound to stick to her resolution.

It was an astonishing situation. When Lucy sat down and tried to think about it coherently, her mind spun into confusion. The whole episode had assumed the unreality of a dream.

She had been at her high desk when the visitors had arrived, and she had dipped a little curtsy as Mr Sawyer paused by her.

'This is Miss Lucy O'Malley, our assistant clerk,' he had said, and the small group of slant-eyed, yellow-skinned gentlemen clustered behind him had bowed politely.

One or two had murmured their names and one taller than the rest had looked at the column of figures in front of her and seemed interested in the neatness of her writing, but after a few minutes they had moved on, and apart from thinking briefly that this was the first time she could recall ever having met any people from China she had dismissed the incident.

When Mr Sawyer had returned that same afternoon to inform her that the mandarin had made an offer for her hand on his son's behalf, she had gaped at him foolishly, half convinced that he was making fun of her.

'The mandarin is anxious to obtain a bride for his son,' Mr Sawyer had repeated impatiently. 'Prince Chang Lee is twenty-six years old and was educated at Oxford, so he speaks English fluently. His father wishes him to marry an English girl, and for some reason he has lit upon you.'

Her employer sounded almost contemptuous at the thought that anyone might consider her worth marrying. It was that tiny flick of contempt that prevented Lucy from refusing the offer at once. Instead, she raised her head, gave her employer a level look, and said,

'What exactly has the gentleman offered?'

'He wished to contact your father but when I explained your er—circumstances he decided that I might be regarded as the proper person to approach,' Mr Sawyer said. 'It is as I have intimated to you. He wishes to obtain an English bride for his son.'

'Cannot the son find his own bride?' Lucy asked.

'Apparently it is quite usual in China for marriages to be arranged through a third party,' Mr Sawyer said. He sounded as if he disapproved of the practice.

'And I would have to live in China?'

'A wife, even in the East, is generally expected to live where her husband resides,' he said.

China was a yellow splodge in her old school atlas with bits of brown to represent the mountains. Lucy had never thought of it as a real place where people actually lived, which was very foolish because there were apparently millions of Chinese busily growing rice and tea and making silk and carving chess sets. They wore big straw hats and baggy trousers and rode about in rickshaws. She had read somewhere that they had discovered gunpowder. She wished she had been more interested in geography in school, but at that time it had never entered her head that she would ever travel very far afield.

'The mandarin requires an answer as quickly as possible as he will soon be returning to China,' Mr Sawyer said. 'Shall I send word to his hotel that you are very grateful for his offer but wish to refuse it?'

'Where in China does he live?' she asked.

'I believe his official home is in Peking, in the Forbidden City.'

Afterwards Lucy decided that it was the thought of the Forbidden City that tipped the balance between acceptance and refusal. She had always been attracted by what was out of reach or considered unsuitable, and the very idea of a place that was actually named as Forbidden woke all the craving for adventure that lay just below her demure surface.

'You may tell him that I shall be very glad to go to China and marry his son,' she said.

Mr Sawyer had felt it his duty to dissuade

her, pointing out that she was very young to take such a drastic step, that the offer of marriage was highly unconventional and not to be even considered by a young woman of sense, and that Miss Peabody would be certain to refuse her consent. Lucy listened, polite but unconvinced, and all the time the words 'Forbidden City' were like a bright light beckoning her out of the greyness of her existence.

'Why, in ten years time, you could be my chief clerk, Miss O'Malley,' he said.

Ten more years of sitting at the high desk and adding up columns of figures. Ten more years of making her way back through the narrow streets to the neat little house where Aunt Harriet had just put on the kettle for tea. In ten years' time she would be twenty-eight years old, and either trapped in a dull marriage or halfway to spinsterhood.

'I have decided to accept the offer,' she repeated firmly. 'Perhaps you'll be kind enough to send word to the gentleman. I must go home and tell my aunt.'

Mr Sawyer had looked as if he regretted very much ever having mentioned the matter to her, but Lucy was already on her way down the stairs.

Walking home slowly through the raw January evening, with the street lights making yellow pools on the half-frozen pavements, she planned her campaign as earnestly as if she were going into battle. From past experience she knew that Aunt Harriet would not be swayed by pleading. The only thing to do was to announce her intentions as calmly as if she had planned a shopping trip to Manchester and to meet objections as they arose.

'My dear, it would take weeks to get to China! And how could you be expected to travel so far all by yourself?'

'There are still tea clippers that make the China run, and they sometimes carry passengers.'

'But not unmarried girls of eighteen! I shall have to consult the vicar!'

When Aunt Harriet consulted the vicar there was no use in arguing. He represented the last court of appeal, and Lucy's heart sank a little as she watched her aunt bring out her church hat of navy felt with the bunch of cherries at the side.

The vicar, however, proved an unexpected ally. He quite agreed that the offer was an unconventional one but in foreign countries different customs prevailed. The Chinese were, according to what he had heard, a highly civilised and artistic race, but if Lucy changed her mind there was nothing in the world to prevent her from turning round and coming straight home.

'But she cannot possibly travel alone,' Aunt Harriet said.

'Of course not. Out of the question!' he agreed promptly. 'However, by great good fortune, that difficulty can be surmounted. It so happens that the Reverend Joseph Willet and his wife are returning to their Mission station in China next month. I had a letter from him only the other day. They had a six months' leave of absence after seven years' service. Now I can inquire the details of their return trip and Miss Lucy could travel back with them. Excellent people both of them. Dedicated to their calling.'

It was clear that Aunt Harriet's hopes of enlisting the vicar as her ally had been dashed, but she took her defeat with good grace, merely remarking that it would be a weight off her mind to know that Lucy was travelling in respectable company.

'And of course there is quite a British colony at the Legation in Peking,' the vicar reminded them as he ushered them out.

'Joseph was telling me that the families of the European diplomats make it a point of honour to keep up Western standards and customs. I believe they even have afternoon tea-parties and a flourishing Ladies Circle.'

'At the very least it will be a most interesting experience,' Aunt Harriet said, as they walked home. 'I must confess I feel easier in my mind since we consulted the vicar, but you must promise me faithfully that if the young man is not sympathetic you will come home at once. You won't allow yourself to be persuaded into a distasteful marriage.'

'I won't do anything I don't want to do,' Lucy said, with the confidence of complete ignorance.

'And you do realise,' said Aunt Harriet, going slightly pink, 'that husbands take certain liberties? One doesn't wish to go into details, but I feel a girl ought to be prepared for experiences that maybe—shall we say embarrassing? Of course many gentlemen are most considerate in such matters, and we must hope that this young man has a certain standard of behaviour.'

Her voice trailed away as she gave her niece an unhappy glance.

'I'm sure we shall manage very comfortably,' Lucy said.

Her voice was calm, but her cheeks had paled a little and her fingers tightened on the strap of her handbag.

Until that moment she had not considered the deeper implications of this marriage at all. She was aware that married people shared the same bed, and she had gleaned sufficient information from the uninhibited conversation of the mill girls to be reasonably certain what went on between the sheets, but she had never connected any of it with herself and the unknown Chang Lee whom she was proposing to marry. Well, she would cross that hurdle when she reached it. To spare Aunt Harriet further embarrassment she began to talk about the clothes she would require.

'It is bound to be warmer in China, so I will need a couple of thin dresses, and I ought to have a good dress in which to be married.'

'Ecru lace over coffee silk would be most becoming,' Aunt Harriet said, effectively diverted. 'With a matching hat, I think. You must allow me to give it to you as a present.'

'That's very kind of you.' Lucy put her hand through her aunt's arm and squeezed it in one of the sudden bursts of affection that characterised her.

'I shall miss you,' Aunt Harriet said, 'and what I shall say to your father if he suddenly arrives I simply cannot imagine!'

'My father hasn't been near us for fifteen years, so he can't complain if we make plans without consulting him,' Lucy said. 'And I'll be coming home to visit, you know, or perhaps later on you could come out to see me. After all, even missionaries get six months off every seven years!'

She had pushed aside the problem of the unknown young man who would be sharing her bed if she went through with the marriage and concentrated instead on the adventure she was certain lay ahead of her. To travel countless miles to a strange land was something she had never pictured as happening to her, and excitement bubbled up in her.

'I do wish we might have been given the opportunity of meeting the gentleman who wished you to marry his son,' Aunt Harriet said when they were eating their supper later. 'It's all very well for him to decide that you are suitable, but I would like to meet the gentleman myself and make up my own mind.'

'He's a mandarin,' Lucy said. 'I think that's a kind of duke, someone important anyway. He probably doesn't consider that he needs checking. His son is a prince, so I suppose that makes me a princess?'

Her green eyes widened as she looked at the other woman.

'Titles are not in the least important,' Aunt Harriet said severely, but Lucy could tell from her expression that the notion of casually mentioning 'my niece, the princess' had begun to soften her disapproval of the whole affair.

'Mr Sawyer sent word to the hotel that I was—favourably inclined towards the marriage,' Lucy said cautiously. 'Perhaps the mandarin will visit us, or invite us to visit him.'

She broke off as a knock sounded at the front door.

'Keep the chain up until you see who it is,' her aunt called as Lucy went through to the narrow hall.

Her niece might be about to leave for China but Aunt Harriet was sure the streets of Oldham were teeming with potential abductors and housebreakers.

'Miss Lucy O'Malley?' The voice was soft and polite, the figure revealed by the gaslight over the door slant-eyed and black haired.

'Yes?'

'My master sends this as a wedding gift with compliments and felicitations,' the man said, bowing and handing her a flat parcel, neatly wrapped in brown paper.

'Oh, won't you come in?' She held the door wider but the man shook his head, bowing again and turning away into the darkness.

'Who is it, Lucy?' Aunt Harriet called.

'The mandarin's servant.' Lucy closed the door and went back into the other room. 'He brought a wedding gift.'

'He certainly takes your acceptance for granted,' her aunt said disapprovingly. 'I think he ought to have brought it by himself.'

'I don't suppose he does anything for himself,' Lucy said.

'You had better open it,' her aunt said, curiosity brimming in her eyes and jerking her fingers towards the string.

'Yes, of course.'

As eagerly as her aunt, Lucy reached for the knots that secured the parcel. The brown paper crackled apart to reveal a flat case of dark wood.

'Lift the lid,' Aunt Harriet said.

For an instant, without knowing why, Lucy hesitated. Until that moment the marriage had been like a dream or a game, but the gift was real and it made the wedding real too. Once she lifted the lid she would be committed to a course of action that led her into the unknown.

Biting her lip, her fingers shaking on the clasp, she raised the lid and stared down at the necklace laid in its nest of dark velvet. It was of twisted silver links with five stones pendant from it. The stones were set in silver but were themselves of a glowing transparency catching the firelight as she lifted the exquisite thing and held it up.

'Moonstones,' Aunt Harriet said, her voice hushed. 'My grandmother had a moonstone brooch once, but it wasn't half as fine as this.'

'It's beautiful,' Lucy whispered.

'A family heirloom, I wouldn't wonder. There's a card with it.'

The white card had the words 'To Lucy, bride of Chang Lee', written on it in a tiny, slanting hand.

'Mr Sawyer said that my fare to China would be paid,' Lucy said, staring at the card. The message on it told her nothing save that the mandarin had not changed his mind about inviting her to become his daughter-in-law. And the necklace was clearly very old and very valuable. But she wished the mandarin had come round himself with the gift instead of sending his servant.

'You'll have to thank him for it,' Aunt Harriet was saying.

'I'll write a note and ask Mr Sawyer to have it delivered to the hotel,' Lucy said.

If the mandarin hadn't troubled to visit her personally then she was determined not to go rushing round to thank him for the necklace.

Yet it was certainly beautiful. Something starved in her nature had been stirred into life by the gleaming stones in their intricate silver setting. She had never owned anything so exquisite in her life. The man she had agreed to marry must be very wealthy. In that case it seemed strange that she should have been chosen as his bride. There was a mystery here which she was not likely to solve until she reached China.

That night when she was in the long-sleeved, high-necked nightdress which Aunt Harriet had pintucked for her, Lucy took the necklace out of its case again and fastened it about her throat. It looked wrong against the pleated yoke of the nightdress and she undid the collar and pulled it off her shoulders, bending to peer into the little square of mirror on the dressing-table.

In the lamplight her flesh glowed creamy and the silver links gleamed and sparkled with little points of fire. The moonstones, nestling in the hollow of her long neck, felt cool but there were depths of colour caught and held in their translucence and her hair, curling about her temples and escaping from its plait, was like strands of fire.

'Prince Chang Lee,' she said softly. The name awoke no echoes, painted no pictures in her mind, but she was almost certain that she could learn to love a man who sent such a gift for his intended bride.

2

Lucy stood on the deck of the ship with Amy Willet and watched the long quayside of Tientsin draw nearer as the vessel edged into harbour. In the pale spring sunshine the choppy little waves made ripples of gold and she cupped her eyes to avoid the dazzle, bringing into focus one of the innumerable small red-sailed fishing-boats that bobbed up and down all around them. A woman with plaits wound round her head and sleeves pushed above her elbows was hauling in a net, her gestures brisk and energetic. She glanced up briefly but it was impossible to tell if she had even noticed the two ladies standing above her.

'I feel that I ought to pinch myself or something to be certain I'm really here,' Lucy said breathlessly.

'Not quite at your destination,' Amy Willet said. 'It will be evening before you reach Peking.'

'I suppose they will send a conveyance for me.'

'I've no doubt of it,' the other answered assuringly. 'I wish Joseph and I were coming with you, but we travel to Langchow.'

The Mission was at Langchow and both the Willets were eager to get back to their duties as quickly as possible. 'Not that our replacement was not an excellent young man, but when the cat's away the mice will play is an adage that might have been invented for our Chinese converts. They are so ready to slip back into superstition and idolatry.'

She was a pleasant little woman, Lucy had found, with an anxious expression on her face. The anxiety was ingrained in her nature and the younger girl suspected that she would have felt quite lost without something to fret about. In contrast, her husband was a man of determined and slightly irritating optimism.

They had proved congenial travelling companions during the weeks of the voyage, lending Lucy a couple of books about China to while away the time and answering her questions as adequately as they could.

'But we know nothing of the Imperial Court,' Amy Willet had said. 'Very few foreigners are allowed into the Forbidden City. The Empress, T'zu Hsi, is reputed to hate Europeans. They call her the Dragon Empress, you know, and her power is absolute. Her nephew, Prince Tuan, is her chief minister, but there are always rumours of plots and counter plots.'

It sounded exciting and faintly sinister. Lucy wondered if she would have the opportunity of meeting the Dragon Empress or her nephew, and if they would disapprove of her because she was a foreigner. The mandarin had apparently approved of her, for he considered her a suitable bride for his son, but she had no idea what position he held in the royal household.

Her formal note of thanks for the moonstone necklace had been duly delivered to the hotel, and Mr Sawyer had handed her an envelope containing sufficient money for her fare.

'One way only,' Aunt Harriet frowned. 'What will you do if you don't like it there?'

'Go to the British ambassador and ask him to lend me sufficient from embassy funds to enable me to get home again,' Lucy said. 'But I'm going out with every intention of liking it there, aunt.'

'I hope you will,' her aunt had said, but her tone had been doubtful.

Events were moving too fast for Aunt Harriet. It had seemed no time at all between Lucy's announcement that she was going to China and the moment when she stood in the narrow hall with her cabin-trunk and her portmanteau at her feet and said,

'Now, don't worry about me. I will send word back every time we reach a port, and a long letter giving you all the news when I get to Peking.'

The Chinese delegation had left, without her having seen the mandarin again. Mr Sawyer told her that he considered the whole business to be most unsatisfactory.

'However, your place here will be kept open for several months, should you wish to return,' he had ended on an unexpected note of kindness. 'I am giving you five sovereigns to keep for any emergencies that might arise. You may regard it as a bonus for the excellent work you have done.'

Lucy had thanked him, said goodbye to the other two clerks, who had shaken hands as sadly as if she were setting off for her own funeral, and walked briskly away from Sawyer's Mill without looking back.

Aunt Harriet and she had indulged in a hasty shopping-trip to Manchester, where her aunt had spent a generous portion of her modest savings on two sprigged cotton dresses, a flowing gown of coffee lace with a wide, veiled hat, and an evening gown of silvery grey silk which was rather low in the neck but which would provide an excellent foil for the moonstones. A travelling dress and coat of soft green wool, two parasols and several pairs of gloves completed the purchases.

'Nobody will be able to say that you didn't arrive with an adequate wardrobe,' Aunt Harriet said.

She spoke fiercely to disguise the lump in her throat and the treacherous moisture in her eyes. She had not felt so emotional since her lively younger sister had gone off to marry her rakish little Irishman. Well, that had ended badly with poor Annie dead of the typhus and her three-year-old child dumped in her lap by her reckless parent. She hoped that this would turn out more happily for the bright-faced girl who was travelling across the world to marry a man she had never even seen.

Lucy had felt a trifle guilty later when

she remembered how cheerfully she had kissed her aunt goodbye. The truth was that she was tense with anticipation and could scarcely wait to begin the journey. The vicar had come to see her off, shaking hands cordially and pressing a Bible into them as he wished her a safe voyage, and then the Willets had bustled up to take care of her, and any last-minute qualms she might have had were swept away in the hooting of the train.

It had taken her several days to find her sea-legs, but once the feeling of dizzy nausea had passed and she had grown accustomed to the occasional pitching and tossing of the vessel, she began to enjoy herself. There were only about a dozen passengers, most of whom would be disembarking at Shanghai. Several of them were missionaries with whom the Willets exchanged anecdotes, and there were two army wives sailing to rejoin their husbands, and a pallid young girl who was taking up a post as governess in Sumatra. Rather to Lucy's surprise her going out to China to marry the son of a mandarin was considered not only mildly eccentric but not quite respectable.

'The Chinese are so very different from

us,' Mrs Arbuthnot said delicately, 'that I would advise you not to rush into anything, my dear. Marriage is such a very final affair.'

She obviously meant to be kind, and Lucy pressed down the little spark of resentment that threatened to flare into temper, and said meekly that of course nothing was settled yet.

Life on board quickly assumed a pattern. Because there were so few passengers the cabin space was better than it might have been, and Lucy had one to herself where she could spread her belongings and retire for privacy. She preferred to spend much of her time on deck chatting with Amy Willet or watching the water slip past, its colour endlessly changing from grey to green to blue and back again, holding a parasol to shield her face from the strengthening sun. Each port of call as they steamed first south and then east was a delight to her. She wished they could have stayed longer so that she could have explored farther inland, but the ship was not a cruise vessel and the passengers had to content themselves with brief glimpses of harbour and shoreline.

They made their own entertainment, the

ladies knitting and playing endless games of cards, the gentlemen playing deck quoits and amusing themselves at a threadbare billiards table in the saloon lounge. The high proportion of missionaries aboard meant regular church services and prayer meetings which at least helped to pass the time. Lucy spent hours reading the books on China, but she suspected the information in them was somewhat out of date. What she would have liked was a book dealing with the customs and culture of the people among whom she was proposing to spend the rest of her life. Without guidance she feared she would make many mistakes in the etiquette of the Imperial household, but her fellow travellers could offer little practical advice.

'The important thing is to keep up one's standards,' Amy Willet said earnestly. 'It is a great temptation to go native as it were, for some of their ways are really quite charming, but one must remember one is there to do the Lord's work and not get carried away into imagining them like us, even if their manners are delightful. The children are enchanting, of course, but they have no idea of the truth. They simply say what they think will please.'

None of that seemed to have much to do with any problems that a girl might face at the court of a foreigner-hating empress. Lucy decided her wisest course of action was to wait and watch, hoping not to make too many blunders along the way.

'We do have an acquaintance at the Legation,' Amy Willet said. 'The son of an old friend of ours is attached to the British Embassy, Stephen Just is his name. It's some considerable time since we met him, but he was a most good-natured person, and I'm sure will be happy to escort you to various functions and introduce you to some nice people.'

'I imagine my husband will escort me,' Lucy began.

'Of course, of course.' Amy Willet looked faintly embarrassed. 'I only meant—if things don't work out as you hope—a friend in a foreign country is such a useful ally, but as you say, no doubt you will be escorted by your er—husband. But if the opportunity arises do make yourself known to Stephen Just. I wish we were coming with you to Peking, but as you know—'

'I shall be perfectly all right,' Lucy said, reassuringly. There was something about the anxious little missionary that seemed to beg for reassurance. Lucy wondered how Amy Willet, with her timid nature, had felt when she first came out to this strange land. The Willets seldom talked about themselves and the nearest that Amy Willet had ever come to making a personal confidence was when she had remarked, with a touch of wistfulness in her voice,

'It is fortunate that we were never blessed with children, for we can devote ourselves to our work without having to worry about other things.'

It would be a wrench to say goodbye to the Willets, Lucy thought, but she could feel the excitement begin to bubble up in her as she strained her eyes towards the shoreline. It looked at this distance very much like any other harbour, crowded with wooden huts and jettys, bales of sacks, coils of rope, and crates being swung up on cranes from the holds of the ships moored along the quay.

The immigration and Customs officials were coming aboard, and the captain had come on deck with his First Officer to meet them and to shake hands with his remaining passengers. Lucy's papers were quickly checked, and she decided she must have imagined the quick glance exchanged between the officials when she stated her destination as the Forbidden City, for a moment later they were bowing and informing her that a conveyance was waiting for her on shore.

'So we really must take our leave of you,' Joseph Willet said, hurrying up to her. 'Leave-taking always has a flavour of regret about it, but I trust we will meet again before too long and, of course, Amy and I will keep you constantly in our prayers. I hope you will think of us too. Our tasks are likely to be more arduous than I had supposed. There has been some trouble in the country districts. Secret nationalist societies. That kind of thing. There were rumours before we went on leave, but we hoped the trouble would blow over. However, we will stand firm, come what may!'

'China is full of secret societies,' Amy Willet said. 'I try not to think about them too much. You will write to us, my dear? The Missionary House, Langchow, will find us. I shall be most eager to hear your news.'

Lucy was promising to write and shaking hands with the captain and then, amid what seemed like a cacophony of shouting and screaming from the porters handling her luggage, she was making her way down the gangplank.

She had half hoped for a ride in a rickshaw, but there was a small wagon with canvas top and sides, drawn by two horses, waiting for her. A man in a dark tunic and trousers, a wide straw hat on his head, approached her. She recognised him as the man who had brought the moonstones and put out her hand impulsively, feeling as if she had met a friend.

Her hand was ignored, the man bowing with his own hands clasped together.

'Welcome, Mrs Lucy,' he said formally, his voice high and singsong. 'I am Chin Shu, servant to the mandarin, Chang Liu. Please to enter the wagon.'

'Yes, of course.' Slightly flustered, she put her own hands together and nodded her head.

The wagon was roomier inside than she had expected and comfortably padded with straps hanging from the roof for the passenger to hold on to. Lucy settled herself on the cushions and leaned to look out of the canvas flap at the side, but there was no opportunity for her to see anything more than a blur, for the wagon rolled forward almost at once, jerking her back against the seat. Evidently Chin Shu was riding on top with the driver. She let the flap fall back into place and resigned herself to a slightly stuffy gloom, hoping that her bags had been strapped on.

They were travelling at a spanking rate, whirling her into an unknown future. At least she had been met, even if neither her future husband nor the mandarin had bothered to come themselves. Once or twice she lifted the flap and glimpsed flat, yellowish land stretching to the horizon. Thick dust swirling up from beneath the wheels made her cough and she leaned back hastily, wiping her stinging eyes with her handkerchief.

After what seemed like days but was probably hours she woke from a half doze to the awareness of light and warm air beating on her closed lids. The wagon had stopped and the flaps of canvas pulled back. Chin Shu stood on the road, holding open the half-door, an expression of resigned patience on his face as if he were prepared to wait all day until she decided to rouse herself.

'Are we there?' Lucy sat upright, clutching at her hat.

'No, Mrs Lucy. Time for food and the changing of the horses,' he said.

'I'll get out,' she said promptly, and shook herself into full wakefulness as she descended into the open.

A sour-faced man, evidently the driver, was unharnessing the horses, and a group of men in shabby tunics and wide-bottomed trousers were grouped a few yards away, staring at her. Lucy half-smiled in their direction, but she had the distinct impression that they moved closer together, whispering shrilly.

'Please to come to the inn, Mrs Lucy.' Chin Shu touched her on the arm, the quick little gesture betraying nervousness.

She went with him across the road, past the whispering men, into a low, thatched building which looked more like a barn than an inn, for it contained only a couple of low tables with benches set down either side of them, and a stove glowing scarlet despite the heat of the day.

'There is a room for washing,' Chin Shu said, indicating a door at the side.

Lucy thanked him and went into the primitive but spotlessly clean bathroom. The water was cold but there was a thick towel, and a small mirror on the wall enabled her to tidy her hair and make sure there were no smears of dust on her face. When she went back into the main room she saw that a small table had been laid and Chin Shu was waiting to serve her. A thin, hot soup with bits of egg in it, some chicken fried with rice, and a dish of green figs comprised the meal. While she ate Lucy noticed that Chin Shu and the sour-faced driver were having their own meal at an adjoining table, and that two or three women hovered shyly in the background. She smiled across at them, nodding to show her appreciation of the food, but their eyes slid away from her and they ducked their heads in embarrassed fashion.

'It is best we leave now, Mrs Lucy,' Chin Shu said, coming up to her. 'Not wise for a European lady to stay too long outside.'

'Is there likely to be trouble?' she asked. 'They were saying something about unrest when we were on board.'

'Not so close to Peking,' Chin Shu said. 'Best to leave now though lest other customers come. Many will not enter if a European is here.'

'But that's silly,' she said.

'Very silly,' he agreed blandly. 'Best we leave now.'

She rose reluctantly, nodding again towards the unresponsive women, and went back to the wagon. Fresh horses were now between the shafts, and the men who had whispered earlier scattered as she emerged from the inn and clustered together again at a little distance. They didn't behave in a very welcoming manner, she thought, with a spurt of annoyance, and turned her head away as she stepped into the wagon again.

The inside of the wagon was dim and even stuffier than it had been before. Now and then she pulled aside the flap and looked out at the dried, yellow landscape with the dust rising from the rough surface of the twisting road. It looked as if it had not rained for months and the sky had a hard, metallic sheen. Once they went through a market-place, the wagon slowing to a crawl as it negotiated the corners of the wooden stalls piled with fruit and vegetables. Lucy held the flap open so that she could see without being seen.

Both men and women seemed to wear the same fashion of high-collared tunics and wide trousers and shallow straw hats and many of the people were barefoot and evidently poor. At the moment their faces looked to her as similar as if they all belonged to the same family, and the shrill chattering she heard sounded like gibberish. She wondered how long it would take her to begin to distinguish between them and to understand something of what they said.

Once through the market-place they picked up speed again, the unsprung body of the wagon jolting uncomfortably and forcing her to hang on to the straps. Lucy had a memory flash of the omnibus at home labouring its way up the steep, cobbled streets. She had always thought that ride a tedious one, preferring to walk to and from the mill, but compared to this rattling contraption the omnibus was luxury indeed.

There was shouting and the sound of running feet, and the wagon stopped so quickly that she was almost flung forward out of her seat. The door was opened and the flaps wrenched aside and she looked out at several men mounted on ponies. The men were Chinese though they looked bigger and broader than the people she had already seen, and they wore a kind of uniform with bright red sashes tied around their waists, and their heads were shaven save for a long pigtail. The man who seemed to be their leader had a drooping black moustache and the sunshine glinted on a carved sabre in his hands. His eyes, black slits in his broad, shiny face, were fixed on her unblinkingly. Lucy stared back at him, determined not to be outfaced, and without moving his own eyes he called out something in a high, sharp tone that made her jump slightly though she couldn't understand the words.

Chin Shu had clambered down from his seat by the driver and answered the man. Lucy thought she discerned the words T'zu Hsi and the man on horseback repeated them in a loud questioning tone and jerked his thumb towards her in a gesture so rude that the blood rushed into her face.

Chin Shu spoke again very rapidly. He was obviously nervous, shuffling from one foot to another, his hands hidden in the wide sleeves of his tunic. The horses stirred restlessly and were checked by the driver.

'What is it? What do these people want?' Lucy demanded, finding her voice.

Chin Shu turned towards her and spoke

rapidly again, but in English this time.

'They demand money before they will allow us to proceed, Mrs Lucy. If we pay them they will escort us to the City.'

'Do we need escort?' she asked.

'It would be wiser to pay them,' he said, 'otherwise we might not reach Peking. These are bad men, Mrs Lucy, and very strong against foreigners. Wiser to pay.'

'Have you got any money?'

'Some gold, Mrs Lucy. Best I give it to them,' he said.

The man was growing impatient, speaking again in a loud voice, running the edge of the sabre between his thick finger and thumb. One of his companions came closer, peering down into the wagon at her. Instinctively Lucy shrank back, a cold trickle of fear running down her spine.

The man laughed and slammed the door shut, edging his horse away and drawing a finger across his throat in an eloquent and terrifying gesture.

Chin Shu was delving into his pocket, and some coins spilled out and lay winking on the dusty road. At once two of the men sprang down and grabbed for the shiny disks, rolling over and over as they struggled. Lucy had a blurred image of

Chin Shu climbing back to his seat, and another of the moustachioed men fingering his sabre, and then the wagon lurched forward faster than it had ever gone before. She clung on to the straps, bracing herself against the violent bumping. She could hear angry shouts and the galloping of hooves behind, but the sounds grew fainter, diminishing into the distance.

The wagon continued its headlong dash and Lucy concentrated grimly on keeping her balance as she lurched from side to side. It was bewildering to be shut up in semi-darkness, with no means of knowing exactly what was happening. Had she been given a choice at that moment she would have turned round and gone straight back to Tientsin where the ship was docked.

The horses slackened speed very gradually and she drew a deep breath, trying to compose herself. Her heart was thudding and the palms of her hands were wet with perspiration. She wiped them shakily on her handkerchief and sat bolt upright, determined to finish her journey with some kind of dignity.

There was another sound now beyond the dim and stuffy confines of the wagon. It came to her ears as a soft, humming noise that swelled and receded like the waves of the sea. She pulled back the flap and risked a hasty glance out, realising almost at once that the noise she could hear was the babbling of many voices, muted by high walls and wooden buildings.

They were approaching a network of streets and squares, crowded with people who jostled one another pitilessly as they bustled about their affairs. The humming had broken up into a hundred separate conversations apparently screamed and shouted across the intervening distances with no thought of privacy. She sat back a little, still holding back the leather so that she could watch the passing panorama. A multiplicity of smells and sounds assaulted her nostrils and eardrums, and a bewildering array of colours flashed past. The Chinese seemed fond of blue and red, and there were yellow banners streaming from the doorposts of many of the buildings.

There were a few shouted remarks as one or two caught sight of her within the wagon, but these people were evidently more accustomed to foreigners, and the wagon rolled on unimpeded. A line of small children in white pinafores crossed the road ahead of the vehicle, marshalled by two nuns. Lucy had a feeling of reassurance when she glimpsed them. In this strange, unwelcoming land children apparently still went to school or for walks supervised by their teachers.

Chin Shu had twisted around on the high seat and was calling down to her. 'Mrs Lucy, we come now to the City. Very soon now we will be at my master's house!'

He sounded as relieved as she felt to be safely at the end of the journey.

Then she glanced ahead and saw, rearing up against the sky, an immense wall of reddish stone in which double doors studded with bronze were set. The wagon stopped and she heard Chin Shu talking to someone. There was the rustling of parchment, an order snapped out, and they were moving forward again as the enormous doors creaked open.

Discarding any remnant of caution Lucy pulled back the flap and took her first look at the Forbidden City. The noise beyond the walls had sunk to a humming again, and the sounds here were gentler. The tinkling of bells mingled with the cooing of doves and the splashing of water into stone fountains set at the corners of the houses. The houses themselves were of stone with conical roofs of yellow tiles. There were little gardens at the sides of the buildings and cherry-trees paraded like brides in long avenues that led from one vast courtyard to the next. Two men, bearing a curtained litter on long poles over their shoulders, went by at a steady, jogging pace. Lucy could see nothing of the occupant but she had the uneasy sensation of being watched by whoever sat concealed within the litter.

The wagon rounded a corner and there was the jangling of harness as the horses were pulled up. Chin Shu descended, opening the half-door and offering his arm to help her step down.

'This is the house of my master,' he said, with a formal bow.

They stood in a small courtyard shaded by a great willow-tree that hung its silvery fronds over a deep pool in which tiny, brilliant fishes twisted and turned. Beyond the courtyard a flight of steps led to an upper courtyard and, beyond that, a great stone house with balconies running its length met her gaze.

A woman was coming down the steps

towards her. Clad in tunic and trousers of pale rose, her black hair skewered on top of her head, she moved gracefully though she was neither slim nor young. When she reached the foot of the stairs she paused, clasping her hands together and bowing.

'Mrs Lucy, I am Chen Sula. I bid you welcome to the House of the Willow,' the woman said.

Her voice was soft, her smile warm, but the eyes raised briefly to Lucy's face were cold, black stones with nothing in them except contempt.

3

For an instant Lucy faltered. She was tired and stiff after the jolting ride in the wagon and this cold-eyed woman seemed to be underlining the fact that she was an unwelcome foreigner in a strange land. And that was ridiculous, because she had come at the mandarin's invitation to marry his son! A decided sparkle came into her green eyes and she said loftily,

'Perhaps you will be kind enough to

show me to my room? I require to rest after my journey.'

Chen Sula bowed again and turned to lead the way up the steps, across the upper courtyard and between slender white columns into the house. Within the hall she paused as if to impress upon Lucy the luxury of her surroundings.

It was a luxury that had its roots in a delicate and charming simplicity. The hall, with its tiled floor and curving stone staircase, had a corridor leading to left and right and an archway hung with silk curtains in a soft, pale yellow. A rug of the same shade covered the floor and the only ornament in the apartment was a vast copper bowl at the foot of the stairs filled with dyed feathers in a variety of brilliant colours.

Chen Sula began to mount the stairs without waiting to see if Lucy was following. Her hand, sliding up the stone balustrade, was adorned with a ring of rose quartz set in a circle of tiny, brilliant diamonds. No servant could possess such a ring, Lucy thought, as she hurried after her, but the woman was surely not a relation of the mandarin's or she would have said so.

The staircase ended in a gallery with corridors to left and right. The floors on this upper storey were carpeted in a thick, dark red with a pattern of tiny yellow dragons, and the doors leading off at each side were of light, polished wood, their frames and panels outlined in red lacquer.

'These are your quarters,' Chen Sula opened a door and went in ahead of Lucy. 'I will have hot water and your luggage brought up for you.'

'You said your name was Chen Sula?' Lucy looked inquiringly at her.

'Housekeeper to the mandarin, Chang Liu,' the woman said.

'Is the mandarin here?' Lucy asked.

'He will return for supper.' Again there came into the black eyes the flick of cold contempt. 'You will wish to change your dress before you meet him.'

'Yes, of course.' Despising herself Lucy said placatingly, 'You speak English very well.'

'It is an ugly language but I made shift to learn it,' Chen Sula said. 'If you will excuse me I will see to the disposal of your bags.'

She made her stiff little bow and glided

out, closing the door behind her. With her going, something dark and brooding lifted from the room. Lucy looked round with interest and pleasure. It was a beautiful apartment, the floor covered with a carpet patterned in various muted shades of blue, curtains of pale apricot silk hanging at the long windows and looped back to the posts of the wide bed. At the foot of the bed was a carved chest, its lid gilded and a matching table was set near to an armless chair piled with blue cushions. Against one wall was an immense wardrobe and, through an inner door, she glimpsed a tiled room with mirrors set round the walls and hip-bath and basin of copper. There was nothing else in the room except a copper bowl, similar to the one in the hall, but filled with tiny yellow chrysanthemums.

Lucy went over to one of the long windows, opened it, and stepped out on to the balcony. As far as she could judge the two wings of the house swept back from the main façade, enclosing between them another courtyard with a fountain in the centre and rows of orange-trees set in tubs along the borders. The courtyard was not enclosed on its third side but became an orchard of cherry and plum feathering the sky. There were steps spiralling down from the balcony to ground level and the air was full of perfume.

Lifting her skirt she went cautiously down the steps. The courtyard was deserted, the windows that faced on to it shuttered against the sun with bamboo screens. The only sound was the splashing of the water in the fountain and the tinkling of wind bells faint and far off in the distance. There was a timeless peace in this place which began imperceptibly to soothe Lucy's ruffled spirits. She went over to the fountain and gazed at it, admiring the graceful curve of white stone down which water flowed and then bubbled up again, sending a fine mist above the rim of the bowl. In the base of the fountain tiny coloured stones had been laid and they moved and shifted as the water cascaded, creating ever-changing patterns.

Lucy walked on into the shade of the trees. It was cooler here, the green paths winding apparently at their own will between trunks round which white-flowered creepers twined. Overhead, little, bright plumaged birds flew in and out of the blossoming branches. It was like the fairyland of which every child dreams, and her heart lifted as she wandered on. The discomforts of the journey and the cold reception afforded her paled into insignificance. In this wood she felt herself to be part of the beauty that surrounded her and not on the outside looking in.

The path widened into a glade and she hesitated at its edge, staring at the building in front of her. It was a pagoda of grey stone, its roof edged with copper from which little bells swung in the breeze. Lichen softened its outlines and carpeted the low step that led up to the door.

Lucy went forward and pushed the door open, peering into the dark interior. It took a moment for her eyes to accustom themselves to the dim green light that filtered through slit windows set high in the walls. The place seemed to be empty save for something that glimmered faintly within an alcove at the other side.

She went forward across the lichen-carpeted floor and stopped, her hand flying to her mouth to suppress a gasp of alarm. Within the alcove a woman lay, one arm under her head, the other trailing over the edge of the couch. The folds of her dress were a brighter green than the light, shielding graceful limbs and a matching veil hid the hair.

The moment of startled unreality passed as Lucy blinked, stepping nearer and bringing the woman into focus. It was not a real person at all but a statue, she realised, and felt foolish as she gazed down at it. Yet her mistake had surely been a natural one. In the dim light the figure looked uncannily lifelike. She leaned closer, marvelling at the delicate beauty of the carving. The figure had been made from some kind of crystal, tinted ivory and green to simulate flesh, and gown, and the couch on which it had been laid was a huge block of onyx set within the wide alcove. The artist had been inspired. Lucy was no judge of excellence but even an inexperienced eye could appreciate the exquisite carving of the delicate girlish features and the skill with which pale gold had been applied to the sculpted waves of the long hair that showed at the edge of the green-tinted veil. Below the hem of the green gown a bare foot revealed itself, each separate nail perfectly delineated. The eyes were closed, the face half hidden by the fall of the veil and in the hand that trailed over the edge of the couch was a branch of willow, fashioned from a carved piece of grey-green jade.

A European woman, Lucy thought in bewilderment, had modelled for this figure. The yellow hair, the features, the rosy tint of the ivory cheeks could never have belonged to an Oriental. Yet this lovingly carved figure had been laid here in this obscure little pagoda where few people were ever likely to appreciate its beauty.

There was a sound behind her and she swung round, every nerve tingling. A shadow moved quickly from the door and then was gone. Lucy stood for a moment, listening, but all she could hear was the tinkling of the small bells hung from the corners of the tiered roof. She was aware suddenly of the loneliness of the place, of her own intrusion into what was clearly a shrine. It was time for her to return to the main house where, no doubt, in due course she would receive answers to the questions crowding into her mind.

She took another look at the peacefully reclining statue and made her way into the open again. There was no sign of the person who had come to the door but on the step lay a yellow chrysanthemum, its petals browning at their tips. She bent and picked it up, smelling the damp, woody scent of the thick stalk. There was a poignancy in that single blossom and she wondered who had come so secretly with a gift of flowers. On impulse she went back into the pagoda and laid the chrysanthemum on the statue, tucking it within the sculptured curve of cheek and elbow. Then she turned and went swiftly out again, closing the door and hurrying along the winding path into the creeper hung trees.

The courtyard, when she reached it, was no longer deserted. A small boy in an embroidered jacket and a round hat was leaning over the rim of the fountain and dabbling his fingers in the water. His chubby face had an absorbed expression and she watched him with pleasure for a moment. Then he looked up and saw her, his eyes widening.

'Good-day to you.' She spoke coaxingly, holding out her hand to him, but he was backing away, shaking his head vehemently.

'The boy believes you will put the evil eye on him,' Chen Sula said, emerging from one of the doors set in the nearest wing. She said something to the child, who immediately ran off with a last terrified glance at Lucy.

'I only wished to make friends,' she began.

'The boy has not seen many foreign faces,' Chen Sula said. 'There is hot water in your room, Mrs Lucy. I didn't know you wished to go for a walk.'

'Only a stroll.' Lucy wished that she didn't have the impression she was expected to apologise. The woman, after all, was only the housekeeper and Lucy was not answerable to her for her actions.

'The gong will be sounded when the mandarin, Chang Liu and Prince Chang Lee return for supper,' Chen Sula said.

Her folded hands and soft voice were the very epitome of a respectful servant but her eyes were still hostile.

'I'll go up and change,' Lucy said, trying to sound as if she were acting entirely on her own initiative.

As she mounted the spiral stairs to the balcony she glanced down and saw Chen Sula still in the courtyard, her hands folded, her eyes turned to watch Lucy's progress. There was something inexorable in that squat, rose-clad figure with the sun glinting on the gold-headed pins that held her black hair in place.

With a feeling of relief Lucy gained her room, closing the window and swishing the curtains across to protect herself from any prying eyes. There was hot water filling the hip-bath and basin, and her cabin-trunk and portmanteau were in the middle of the room. She was glad that nobody had begun to unpack for her. Her new clothes were elegant enough to be seen by anybody, but she disliked the idea of Chen Sula's fingers handling them.

It was marvellous to divest herself of her travelling dress and undergarments and sink into the comfort of hot water clouded with fragrant oil. There were sponges and towels and cakes of soap within easy reach, and when she finally stepped out on to the fleecy bathmat she was confronted, for the first time in her life, with her own naked image reflected in the full-length mirrors. Her eyes were wide as she stared at herself. It was like looking at a stranger, a pale-skinned, high-breasted girl with curving thighs and legs that were long for her height. Her red hair, its ends curling damply, was tied on top of her head and there was a sprinkling of freckles across her nose despite all

Aunt Harriet's ministrations with lemon juice and buttermilk. The girl in the mirror looked like a nymph poised on the threshold of a new experience with some woodland satyr, her lips parted in expectation, a flush of desire mantling her cheeks.–

With a little shock of embarrassment Lucy came down to earth, wondering where on earth her mind had wandered as she gazed at herself. It was time to dress and coil up her hair. She was not certain how formal the supper was likely to be, but it would be a graceful acknowledgement of the mandarin's gift if she wore the moonstones and that meant wearing the evening dress. It certainly looked effective, she decided, when she had hooked up the tight, low-cut bodice and smoothed the silvery-grey silk over her hips. Against her bare skin the necklace glowed with a life of its own, the twisted silver links catching the last rays of the sun. She arranged her hair in a loose coil and slipped on the low-heeled silver sandals that she had bought to complement the outfit.

The gong had not yet sounded. To fill in time she unpacked her remaining clothes and hung them in the wardrobe.

The dresses occupied only a narrow space and even when she had laid her new lace-trimmed nightdress across the bed and put the Bible the vicar had given her on the table, the room held little trace of her personality. She was still a foreigner in this lovely room. Only in the wood and in the pagoda where the statue slept had she felt herself to be more than a stranger.

A dull booming noise reverberated through the silent house. Although she had been listening for it the actual sound made her jump violently. In a very few moments she would come face to face with the man whom she had agreed to marry. The decision made so impulsively in the cold of a January day had brought her to this exotic place, to give her heart and hand to a man she had never seen. At that instant she found herself wishing passionately that she was back in Oldham, on her way home from Sawyer's Mill to spend a quiet evening with Aunt Harriet.

The gong boomed again and she drew a deep breath, straightening her shoulders. It would do her no good at all to cower here in her room. Slowly she moved towards the door, opened it and went into the long corridor. The other doors were all closed, but oil-lamps hung at intervals from sconces in the wall. It was not quite dark but the colour was going out of the world, and the lights imparted a cheerfulness to the little yellow dragons that rollicked along the red carpet.

In the gallery she paused, looking over the white stone railing to the hall below. Oil-lamps had been lit here too and from the partly opened door of an inner room voices floated up to her. They were male voices, speaking Chinese, and their tone was angry. Lucy went down the stairs, wishing she felt more confident. This meeting would be difficult as it was, and the prospect of walking in on a violent family quarrel would make matters infinitely worse.

There was nobody to announce her, but evidently her step had been heard on the tiled floor, for the voices abruptly ceased. Lucy pushed the door wider and stood on the threshold of a long room furnished with deceptive simplicity in yellow and pale biscuit shade. She had an impression of low tables and curved chairs and ivory figures set on a shelf along the wall. Then her eyes moved to the mandarin.

She would not have recognised the dark-suited gentleman who had visited the mill in this scarlet-gowned figure who stepped forward with his hands clasped together and bowed.

'Welcome to the House of the Willow, my daughter,' he said formally. 'I was pleased to learn that you had arrived safely.'

'Not so safely,' she said. 'We were stopped on the way from Tientsin by some men who wanted us to pay money for protection.'

'Chin Shu told me about the incident. It was most unfortunate, but these Boxers are getting very bold. I had not heard of them so close to the city before.'

'Boxers?' She wrinkled her brow in puzzlement.

'That is merely the nickname given to them,' the mandarin said. 'They belong to the Society of the Fists of Righteous Harmony. A nationalist secret society, but you need not bother your head about them. You must come and meet my son now. This is a private occasion, so we will dispense with the formalities. Lee, come and make your bow.'

His voice had sharpened slightly and

there was a faintly warning note in it.

Lucy had been acutely conscious, throughout the brief exchange, of the tall figure who stood in the shadows, staring through the window. His back was towards her and she could see only the tightly clenched hands and the rigid set of the broad shoulders. What emanated strongly from the man was a sense of burning, quivering resentment and, as he turned slowly and stepped into the lamplight, she braced herself as if she expected a blow.

She had not tried consciously to build up any picture of the man she was to wed, but she had a dim idea of someone who looked exactly like the mandarin but younger. The man facing her however looked more European than Oriental, his black hair cut in shaggy locks that were short by Chinese standards and long by English ones, his black eyes tilted above high cheekbones. His high-necked tunic and trousers were of black silk faced with scarlet and in his belt was a curved dagger, its handle studded with rubies.

'Miss Lucy.' He spoke her name as if he were forcing it through his teeth.

'You don't look Chinese,' she blurted, and stopped, aware that the hot anger in the man had suddenly become icy rage.

'I am Eurasian. Thank you for reminding me,' he said, and the bitterness of his voice shocked her.

'My late wife was a Frenchwoman,' the mandarin said without expression.

'Oh, then—' Lucy hesitated, wondering whether to mention her visit to the pagoda, but before she could make up her mind the mandarin said, 'Shall we go into the dining-room? Lucy must be hungry.'

The dining-room adjoined the apartment where they were standing and was more European in feeling, the long table set with crystal and porcelain and silver, an immense dresser along one wall holding a vast array of silver and crystal. Two soft-footed servants moved in and out with covered dishes of silver. There seemed to be a great many courses, all served at the same time, from which the mandarin and his son helped themselves frequently in small amounts. Somewhat nervously Lucy followed suit, enjoying the unfamiliar flavours and textures of the spicy fish, and meat, and lightly cooked vegetables. At the other side of the long table Chang Lee ate silently, ignoring her, but his father, who sat between them at the head of the table, seemed to feel it incumbent on him to supply an endless stream of gently rambling conversation about his recent trip to England.

'A most interesting journey. It is many years since I left China and I found the experience invigorating. My son, of course, was educated in England and is already acquainted with London, and many other large cities. There are new techniques in the spinning and weaving of cotton, of course, which might be employed here with advantage.'

'Do you have a mill, sir?' She dragged her eyes from the brooding gaze opposite and asked the question politely.

'No. I merely went to investigate the methods used in English mills so that a full report might be prepared for the Empress. She is aware of the necessity to increase employment in China.'

'Surely the Europeans bring trade,' she ventured.

'That is true, but we import too much,' the mandarin said. 'Such a vast country as ours should be self-supporting. In that, at least, I agree with the Nationalists. What troubles the Empress is that our own customs and traditions are being eroded by foreign influence.'

'She is reputed to hate foreigners,' Lucy said.

'I fear her experience of them has been very unfortunate,' he answered. 'The opium trade is controlled by Europeans, and that has brought no benefit to China.'

The servants had brought in small bowls of candied fruits and the mandarin was pouring wine for her. Glancing from under her lashes Lucy tried to study Chang Lee's face, to catch some glimmer of friendliness in his remote expression. He was eating and drinking as if he sat alone, and her heart sank a little. She had wondered if she would be willing to go through with the marriage, but it had never entered her head that he would reject her. The thought was a sobering one.

'Your bride is an intelligent young lady,' the mandarin remarked. 'She was most highly regarded by her employer.'

'I will remember that when I require any accounts balancing,' Chang Lee said.

There was no escaping the hostility in his voice. The colour rose in Lucy's face and her temper bubbled up.

'I imagine a husband would expect more

than that from a wife, just as a wife would expect more from a husband,' she said sharply.

'You would be wise to expect nothing at all,' he said. It was the first time he had addressed her directly since they had sat down to eat, and the icy indifference in his voice added fuel to her own fury. Raising her head she fixed stormy green eyes on him and said, her voice trembling, 'I expected courtesy, for which I was given to understand the Chinese are renowned! It was no easy thing to leave my own home, and trail all the way here, but I'd not have you think yourself bound by any arrangement that has been made. I'm sure my passage home can be arranged if you don't wish to go through with the marriage—'

She was interrupted. Chang Lee, his voice harsh, broke in.

'Go through with the marriage! My dear Miss Lucy, we are already wed!'

'What? I don't understand how—I wasn't there,' she said childishly.

'We were married by proxy,' he said, and his hard mouth twitched as if he derived an unwilling amusement from her look of consternation. 'A week ago, in the Winter

Palace, with the Empress herself as witness. A simple but moving ceremony. One of the Court eunuchs played your part.'

'But surely—is that legal?' she gasped.

'Perfectly legal,' the mandarin said. His eyes were lowered and his long fingers beat a nervous tattoo on the edge of the table. 'You are now Princess Chang Lucy.'

'But don't let it trouble you,' Chang Lee said. 'It is not my intention to inflict myself on you more than custom demands. There are some matters that not even the Empress may order!'

4

Lucy woke to the tinkling of the wind bells and the cooing of doves outside the window. For a moment she lay confused, wondering how she had come to be in this wide, silk hung bed. Then memory flooded back and she sat up, her red hair tumbling over her shoulders. She was in the Forbidden City, already married to a Eurasian prince who obviously hated the whole affair but had agreed to it for some obscure reason of his own.

'You're so sharp you'll cut yourself one of these days,' had always been one of Aunt Harriet's stock sayings.

There was some truth in that, Lucy thought ruefully. She had agreed to the mandarin's fantastic offer because she was bored with her job in Sawyer's Mill and craved more excitement than her life in Oldham afforded, but she had not thought deeply about the step she was taking because, at the back of her mind, she had been certain that she could turn round and go home again if she wished. Now it looked as if she had been caught in the net that she herself had helped to weave. The meal had ended in an embarrassed silence, and she had excused herself as soon as she could and gone to her room.

Rather to her own surprise she had fallen asleep almost at once, her last conscious thought being the resolve to visit the British Legation as soon as possible. An unconsummated marriage could surely be annulled, even in China. And then she had known nothing more until the sun had laid a rod of gold across her pillow.

There was a tap at the door and the two little maid-servants entered. One carried hot water and the other a tray of tea and fragrant cinnamon rolls, in their tunics and trousers with their plaits strained back so tightly from their foreheads that both wore expressions of perpetual surprise, they looked like dolls. She addressed them loudly and slowly, hoping they would understand.

'Good morning, and thank you!'

One of them giggled, putting her hand to her mouth, and shaking her head. The other, however, gave the customary bow and said in a sweet, tinkling voice that had in it all the fugitive charm of the windbells.

'Missy Lucy, good morning. You sleep good?'

'Very good—I mean well. What's your name?'

'Yang Fei, Missy. My sister is Yang Chi, but she no speak English.'

'There was a little boy in the courtyard yesterday,' Lucy remembered. 'Do you know who he was?'

'Boy?' Something like a shutter closed in the narrow face. 'Many childs in Peking, Missy. Under your feets.'

Lucy was about to pursue the point, but the other girl had turned. Her eyes were fixed on the bowl of yellow chrysanthemums.

'They're lovely, aren't they?' Lucy said brightly, pushing back the bedcovers and preparing to rise. The girl was shaking her head again.

'Ching Ming blossom,' Yang Fei said.

'What is Ching Ming?' Lucy inquired.

The two girls looked at each other uncertainly. Then Yang Fei said, her face grave,

'Ching Ming is Feast of the Dead, Missy Lucy. These are flowers taken to the dead. It must be a—mistake to have them put in this room.'

It was no mistake, Lucy thought. She was quite sure that Chen Sula had placed the bowl of chrysanthemums in her room, and no doubt derived a twisted pleasure from the knowledge that such flowers were intended for the dead.

'Am I to take them, Missy?' Yang Fei asked.

'Leave them. I'll see to them myself,' Lucy said slowly.

They bowed themselves out, closing the door softly. Lucy ate the breakfast and drank the tea. The maids had evidently forgotten the milk and sugar, or perhaps they drank it like this in China with a slice of lemon laid in the saucer.

She washed and put on one of the new gowns of sprigged cotton, braiding back her hair and tying a scarf over it.

When she opened the window and stepped out on to the balcony the courtyard below was deserted. She took the bowl of chrysanthemums and descended the spiral stair, passing the fountain, and walking quickly into the orchard. For a moment the paths confused her, but she lit on the right one almost at once and threaded her way between the creeper-hung trees towards the glade. The little pagoda looked even more lonely today, its copper-edged roof scarcely touched by the sunshine that filtered with difficulty through the leaves.

She pushed open the door and went in, blinking as she accustomed her eyes to the gloom. The lady lay still in the alcove, like some maiden sunk in an enchanted sleep. The flower that Lucy had placed there drooped with browning petals where she had left it, but other flowers had been woven into a wreath and fitted carefully on the veiled head. Lucy moved to the end of the onyx block and set down the bowl of chrysanthemums on the lichened floor. It was then that she noticed the inscription cut into the stone, each letter delicately gilded, and bent closer, tracing the symbols with her finger.

Princess Chang Marie
1856–1880

It must be Chang Lee's French mother who lay here. She had died at the age of twenty-four, leaving a child of six. But the carving must surely have been executed when she was alive. She must have posed for it, taking her place day after day while the artist shaped and tinted the crystal.

Lucy shivered, imagining what it must be like to lie here in this forgotten place. Yet not quite forgotten as the wreath of little yellow chrysanthemums bore mute witness.

As she came out into the glade she caught a flash of red disappearing into the trees. It was no more than a momentary glimpse, but she was certain she had recognised the small boy she had seen in the courtyard the previous day. She followed him, stumbling over the path as it grew rougher and narrower, the trees arching together high above her head.

The path ended in a flight of steps that curved up into a small, paved courtyard.

There were peach-trees here, set in a long line beneath the whitewashed walls of a house. Two shuttered windows stared down at her, like eyes with the lids slyly lowered. The entrance was doubtless round the other side of the building. There was a wrought-iron gate set in the courtyard wall.

Something at the left-hand window moved and a corner of the blind was twitched aside. Looking up, Lucy could see a hand, its fingers curling about the edge of the bamboo. A ring on the finger flashed fire into her eyes, but the rest was in shadow.

There was something unpleasant about being spied upon, and Lucy stared back defiantly. The red-clad child had vanished, but she fancied now that she had heard the clanging of the gate, and turned towards it with the intention of finding her way to the main entrance. There was a sudden furious barking and something hurled itself against the bars. Lucy stepped back hastily, glad that there was a barrier between her and the yellow-maned creature that snarled at her, its fangs bared, its barking dying into an even more ferocious growl.

There was no hope of passing the dog.

With what dignity she could muster, Lucy retraced her steps, resisting the temptation to look up at the window. She was sure that the unseen person who held back the blind watched her retreat with amusement. The fear that someone might open the gate and release the snarling beast made her hurry despite her resolve, and she found to her annoyance that she was panting when she reached the courtyard of the mandarin's house.

She spent a few minutes tidying her hair and then made her way down the inner staircase to the hall. As there seemed nothing particular that she was expected to do, now seemed as good a time as any to explore. The curtained archway opposite the main door led into a large room with a colonnade of pillars supporting arched windows that led into the courtyard. The pillars were of greenish grey stone, the walls painted in the same shade, the floor a mosaic of red and gold. This was evidently a formal reception room, furnished with high-backed chairs and low stools and tables. In one corner, poised in a niche, was the ivory figure of a tree, its branches tinted green. Lucy went nearer and saw, as she looked more closely, that a figure was emerging from the trunk of the tree. The head and shoulders of a slant-eyed girl were growing out of the tree, or forming part of it. It was difficult to tell if the girl was part of the bark or escaping from its confines.

'That is the girl of the Willow,' Chang Lee's voice said from the door.

'There must be a story to it,' she said, half-turning as he crossed the floor towards her.

'An old family legend,' he said. 'My father tells it better than I do. There was a young man, so the tale goes, who vowed he would never marry until he met a maiden who had no fault in her. His relations laughed at him, saying his dream was an impossible one, but he prayed to the Mother Goddess, to Kwan Yin, to grant his wish. And Kwan Yin heard his prayer and threw down to him a branch of willow, telling him to plant it in his garden. So he planted the branch and watered it and it grew into a fine tree. But then a beautiful girl came to the Forbidden City, and Chang Liu, the young man, fell so deeply in love with her that he forgot his vow and took her as his wife though she was full of faults. It was a happy marriage, with many children, but he always sensed there was something missing in his life. He never knew exactly what it was, but when his spirit was troubled he would go to the willow-tree and sit in the shade of its branches and be soothed. He never knew that in the tree was the maiden without sin whom Kwan Yin had sent to him in the form of the willow branch, but then he had never looked properly at the tree and so the maiden was held there by his own blindness.'

'What happened?' she breathed.

'Oh, he eventually grew old and died, but the maiden lived on in the willow and lives there still, for she had been created for love and only love can free her or give her rest.'

'That's a beautiful story, but a very sad one,' she said, as he finished his narrative.

'There are many legends in China.' He gave a shrug, the bitterness returning to his face. 'Superstitions, many would say.'

'My Aunt Harriet says there is often a core of truth in the most unlikely tale.'

'Your Aunt Harriet?'

'My mother's sister. She brought me up after my mother died and my father—went away,' she explained.

'In Lancashire?'

'In Oldham,' she nodded. 'Have you ever visited Oldham?'

'Mercifully, no.' His mouth twitched again slightly.

'So you can understand why I was pleased to have the opportunity of coming to China,' she said evenly.

'I was extremely rude to you last night,' he said abruptly. 'My father was right to admonish me later. Courtesy is always due to a guest, else the shame falls upon the family of the host, and you did come at my father's invitation.'

'I didn't know that we were already married,' she hesitated. 'I thought we would be given time to make up our minds.'

'It was the wish of the Empress.'

'That you should marry me?' She blinked at him. 'How could she have heard of me, and what business is it of her's, anyway?'

Chang Lee shot her a brief, ironic glance and laughed shortly.

'The Empress T'zu Hsi makes it her business,' he said. 'She knows everything that goes on in the Forbidden City, and she has absolute dominion over its inhabitants.

You would do well to bear the fact in mind.'

'I walked in the orchard this morning,' Lucy said. 'I saw the pagoda and the statue of—would it be your mother?'

'Yes.'

Just the curt monosyllable, but she felt as if a door had been slammed in her face. While she tried to think of some way of continuing the conversation without blunder Chang Lee bowed, saying in the sharp, hostile manner of the previous night, 'Excuse me, but I have other matters to attend.'

He went out without waiting for her reply, and she was left in the handsome apartment with the distinct impression that she had been snubbed. Glancing at the carving again the thought crossed her mind that in style it was like the statue in the pagoda, and might have been executed by the same hand. It was futile to speculate, and she would think twice before she asked Chang Lee any questions concerning it. He had met her in a friendly mood and then, as soon as she had mentioned the pagoda he had behaved as if she had committed some unforgivable breach of etiquette. Lucy sighed, thinking it was a great pity that they couldn't establish some kind of friendship. He was an undeniably attractive man with that interesting blend of Chinese and European in his features, and when he had smiled at her she had been conscious of a fluttering sensation beneath her tight bodice.

Abruptly she shut off her train of thought and went out into the hall again, turning this time into the wing she had not yet seen. A curtain of bamboo shielded the passage from the hall, and there was the inevitable chiming of wind bells as she went past. These were evidently the kitchen quarters, for when she pushed open a nearby baize-covered door she was greeted by a buzz of high-pitched chatter and the clattering of pans. Several people were engaged in cutting up vegetables at a long table and washing them in a stone sink that ran almost the length of the room. She could see bulging sacks and long strings of tiny red onions and green peppers.

Gradually the chatter ceased and six or seven pairs of eyes focused on her unwaveringly. Lucy had the impression that without actually moving they had all taken a step backwards. A little uncertainly she put her hands together and bowed her head, and one or two of them followed suit and promptly broke into nervous tittering.

'Good morning.' Her voice came out too loudly and somewhere a pan clattered against the edge of the sink. Lucy stepped to the table, picked up what looked like a bit of celery and put it into her mouth, nodding and smiling as she did so to indicate her appreciation of whatever she was chewing. She felt a perceptible relaxing of the atmosphere and a small, wrinkled woman who sat in the corner shelling peas into a dish said something to her in a quavering and gentle old voice.

There was a footfall in the passage and Chen Sula came in. Her tunic and trousers were of pale blue this morning and there was a blue band wound about her top knot of black hair. At her entrance the servants began their work again with a vigour that would have been comical if it had not had about it the smell of fear.

'Mrs Lucy!' The thin brows rose in slight but unmistakable reproof. 'I did not know you wished to inspect the servants' quarters or I would have made arrangements for you to be escorted round.'

'Oh, I like to wander around by myself,' Lucy began.

'Perhaps you would be kind enough to inform me another time,' Chen Sula said, holding back the door.

If she stayed to argue she would probably end by making a fool of herself. Lucy went out slowly, aware that her cheeks were burning and her fists tightly balled.

'The servants are nervous,' Chen Sula said as they walked back into the hall. 'I'm afraid they regard all white people as foreign devils. It would be much better if you let me know when you want to go into the kitchens again.'

'What about your late mistress?' Lucy was driven to ask. 'She was a Frenchwoman, I believe?'

'Yes, Mrs Lucy.'

'And did she have to give warning every time she wanted to go into her own kitchen?' Lucy inquired.

'As mistress of the mandarin's house she was not in the habit of going to the servants' wing,' Chen Sula said.

'Oh.' Lucy felt suitably crushed by the coolly insulting tone.

'I came with a message for you, Mrs Lucy,' the housekeeper continued.

'Yes?' Swallowing her annoyance Lucy gave an inquiring look.

'The Empress has sent word that she wishes you to attend her this afternoon,' Chen Sula said. 'Her Imperial Majesty will grant you a private audience in the Winter Palace. We had not expected such a summons for weeks, so it is a signal honour for you to be received so quickly.'

'Is it?' Lucy felt somewhat doubtful.

'A litter will be sent for you at three o'clock,' Chen Sula said. 'Perhaps you would care to lunch early and allow yourself sufficient time in which to make yourself presentable?'

'Yes. Yes, very well.' Lucy frowned slightly, disliking the other's choice of words. 'The mandarin—'

'The mandarin, Chang Liu, and Prince Chang Lee went out for the remainder of the day,' Chen Sula told her. 'The audience is to be a private one, but if you are afraid I shall be very willing to accompany you.'

'Thank you, but I shall go alone,' Lucy said coldly.

'I would suggest a high-necked gown and a hat,' Chen Sula went on. 'The Empress is known to value modesty in women.'

'Thank you,' Lucy said again, helpless

before the older woman's calm assumption of authority.

'I took the liberty of setting a cold lunch for you,' Chen Sula said.

It was in the elegant dining-room, laid at one end of the long table. To Lucy's dismay Chen Sula remained to wait upon her, drawing out one of the high-backed chairs and pouring a light, dry wine into the crystal goblet at her right hand. The various dishes of shellfish and small pieces of cold meat were served with a variety of subtle sauces and there were slices of melon and juicy peaches for dessert. Lucy tried to concentrate on the meal but she was conscious of the silent presence of the Chinese woman.

It was Lucy who broke the silence, though she had resolved not to be the first to do so.

'Have you worked for Chang Liu for a long time?'

'I came into the household when I was nine years old,' Chen Sula said. 'That was in the year of the sickness—a fever which killed the other members of my family. The mandarin was a young man of nineteen then.'

'And that was?'

'Thirty-three years ago,' Chen Sula said.

So she was only in her early forties. Lucy doing quick calculations in her head, had thought her older, but perhaps Chinese women aged more quickly.

'When did—when was the mandarin wed?' she asked.

'Twenty-eight years ago. He had visited Indo-China and he came back with a French wife, a missionary's daughter.'

'The Princess Chang Marie.' She fancied the other gave a slight start and added,

'I visited the pagoda in the wood.'

'It would be wiser if you did not mention your visit to the mandarin,' the housekeeper said. 'The pagoda is not visited these days. Was there anything else you wanted to find out?'

'Not at the moment,' Lucy spoke evenly, meeting the woman's cold eyes with indignant green ones.

'Then if you will excuse me I will have hot water taken up to your room.'

The woman gave her a frigid little bow and went out, plump hips swaying slightly under the blue tunic.

It was clear that, just as she resented Lucy's presence, so she had resented the mandarin's wife. That didn't explain the isolated and neglected pagoda, nor the yellow chrysanthemums wreathed so carefully round the head of the statue.

When she entered her room she found Chen Sula there, laying out the gown of coffee-coloured lace and the wide, creamy hat with its trimming of lace.

'For the audience with Her Majesty,' she indicated. 'There is hot water in the bathroom, Mrs Lucy, and I will send Yang Fei to put up your hair. She has clever fingers, though not much sense in her head.'

'One other thing,' Lucy paused, drawing a deep breath.

'Yes, Mrs Lucy?'

'That's what I wished to speak to you about,' Lucy said firmly. 'I was not aware of it when I arrived, but Prince Chang Lee and I were apparently wed by proxy before I reached Peking. And that makes me Princess Chang Lucy, not Mrs Lucy. Perhaps you would be kind enough to remember that.'

She had screwed up her courage to issue the reproof, but she was not ready for the implacable hatred that flared into Chen Sula's black eyes. For a moment she feared that the woman would actually strike her as the black head reared up.

'As you say, you are now the Princess Chang Lucy,' Chen Sula said, biting off each word as if it were a length of thread. 'Excuse me, please.'

Turning, without troubling to bow, she went out, closing the door so gently that Lucy knew she had been strongly tempted to bang it violently.

Lucy shivered, chilly despite the warmth of the room. She felt somewhat calmer when she had washed and put on the gown of coffee lace. It was ironic that she had chosen the dress for her wedding and would now wear it to be inspected by the Empress who hated foreigners and yet had apparently decreed that one of her courtiers must marry one.

Certainly she would have made a lovely bride, she thought ruefully. The dress on its foundation of silk had a high, ruched neck and ruffles on the elbow sleeves. More ruffles edged the hem of the flowing skirt and the matching shoes were of soft brown leather.

There was a tap at the door and Yang Fei came in, making her neat little bow.

'You wish your hair to be done, Mrs Lucy?' she questioned politely.

'Princess Chang Lucy. Did you know that Chang Lee and I were wed?'

'We heard the tale, but Madam Chen Sula said—' The girl hesitated.

'Madam Chen Sula said what?' Lucy sat down, submitting to the other's ministrations.

'That you might go away again. Not stay long,' Yang Fei said, looking embarrassed.

'Oh, I will probably be staying,' Lucy said.

'Plin-Princess then. The word is hard for me.'

Yang Fei began to coil Lucy's hair into an elaborate chignon at the nape of her neck. Her fingers were both gentle and nimble and the girl felt herself relaxing. At least this little servant was not part of the general hostility.

'Were the others afraid when I went into the kitchen?' she asked on impulse.

'A little. Some of them fear the evil eye when it is cast on them by foreign devils,' Yang Fei said.

'But you are not?'

'I went to the Mission School in Peking for three years,' the girl said.

As she gained confidence so her command of English was improving.

'But your sister didn't go?'

Yang Fei shook her head. 'She was not strong to learn much,' she said, 'but I like to learn.'

'I would like to learn Chinese,' Lucy confided.

'Many tongues in China. Mandarin is used at the Court.'

'Then I will learn Mandarin. Will you teach me?'

'To speak a little, yes. I cannot read or write it. Many scholars spend many years in the learning of Mandarin,' Yang Fei said earnestly. 'You will stay here such a long time?'

'I might,' Lucy smiled at the girl and nodded her approval of the hairstyle.

'Come! I will help you cover the red with the big hat,' Yang Fei said. 'In China the red hair is not good to have. Bad luck.'

'Is that so?' Lucy took another look at her reflection in the mirror.

'I think you are a pretty lady,' Yang Fei said kindly. 'For a foreign devil, very pretty indeed!'

'Thank you, Yang Fei,' Lucy rose and reached for the wide-brimmed hat, tying the brown ribbons under her chin.

'You will take care in the palace of the

Empress?' the girl said. 'It is said her mind and temper can blow like the wind.'

'I'll take care.' Lucy smiled at her, and went out, drawing on the long cream gloves that matched the hat.

In the hall the manservant, Chin Shu, hurried forward, his hands clasped together, an expression of great anxiety on his face.

'Please to hurry, for the royal litter is come,' he begged.

'I'm quite ready.' Lucy took another deep breath and walked out across the upper courtyard, down the steps, and past the drooping grey-green branches of the willow. In the street a litter, hung with scarlet silk and fringed in gold, had been set down, and a pigtailed man, clad in a long red robe, waited to hand her inside.

5

For the first time in her life she was riding in a litter, as if time had sped backwards from the dawn of the twentieth century to the mediaeval age. Had she not been so nervous she would have enjoyed the experience more, imagining herself to be some great lady out of the history books, but she was too much aware of the reality that lay ahead. T'zu Hsi wished to inspect the foreign devil that Chang Liu had found as a bride for his son. And T'zu Hsi hated foreigners.

The bearers of the litter had set up a steady trotting pace that was much more comfortable than the jolting wagon had been. Through the slits in the red curtains Lucy had brief glimpses of yellow-roofed, white stone houses, a woman hurrying along with a small child strapped to her back and a large bowl of fruit balanced on her head, a cherry-tree flinging pink blossom into the sky. There was great beauty in this city and she wished she had the tranquillity of mind to appreciate it properly.

They passed through a series of red-lacquered doors gilded with huge dragons and down long passages open to the sky. A flock of white doves rose from some hidden nest and everywhere the bells tinkled.

The litter was set down and a tall Chinese, his robe embroidered with the inevitable dragon, helped her to alight. To her relief he spoke in English.

'Please to accompany me? I am Sung Li, official interpreter to Her Imperial Majesty T'zu Hsi.'

'How do you do?' Lucy was not sure whether to offer her hand, but Sung Li had already bowed and was leading the way down a short corridor to high red doors which opened silently at their approach.

Her first impression was of a splendour so opulent that it barely escaped vulgarity, a huge golden dragon swished its tail and belched fire in the centre of a mosaic of red, blue and green. The walls were hung with curtains of yellow silk and there were ivory chairs, their seats upholstered in velvet. Tall vases of gold and crystal held sprays of white blossom and against one wall a carved screen was inlaid with cool jade and lapis lazuli.

There was no time for Lucy to absorb any details of the enormous apartment. Her eyes flew almost at once to the dais at the farther end. Below the dais a semi-circle of officials in long tunics of red and green and blue were standing with their hands folded within their wide sleeves, but the dais itself was dominated by a high throne of dull green jade, its arms carved into dragon heads set with ruby eyes and tongues and sprayed with gold dust. There was a figure seated on the throne, a squat figure clad in a long robe of gold.

The interpreter touched Lucy's arm and they moved forward towards the motionless, unblinking figure. At the foot of the dais Sung Li prostrated himself at full length, burying his head in his arms. For an astonished instant she feared that she was expected to follow suit.

'And I wouldn't grovel on the floor for Queen Victoria herself,' the girl thought. She compromised by clasping her hands together and bowing her knee.

The Empress said something in a high, surprisingly sweet voice, and Sung Li rose, folding his hands within his sleeves and answering. He was evidently giving Lucy's name, for the Empress said something else and he turned to help Lucy to her feet.

'The Empress bids you welcome and asks if your journey was a pleasant one,' he said.

'Please tell Her Majesty that my journey was most interesting,' Lucy said again.

Sung Li spoke again, bowing deeply as he did so. Lucy's eyes were fixed upon the Empress, and in her mind rose the uneasy comparison of a rabbit hypnotised by a snake. T'zu Hsi had snake eyes, small, black, unblinking, in a wide yellow face and her black hair was puffed out like the head of a cobra. Her hands, resting along the carved dragon heads, were surprisingly delicate, their two-inch-long fingernails protected by jewelled sheaths. The robe of cloth of gold fitted closely to the dumpy figure and the mouth was a straight line.

There was nothing beautiful about the Empress save her surroundings, but there was power radiating from her. Lucy could almost touch it, so strong was its force, and she found it hard to repress a shudder of fear as she met the implacable gaze of the old woman.

T'zu Hsi nodded her head and said something else. Two of the officials went to her at once, placing their hands under her elbows, helping her to rise. Lucy took an involuntary step backwards as the figure descended the three steps of the dais. Seen at close quarters the Empress T'zu Hsi was like some obese heathen idol, the face without gentleness, the skin putted with tiny lines, and she was old. It would have been impossible to guess her age, for she moved slowly and stiffly but the hands were young and the snake eyes bright with intelligence and malice.

They were moving towards the carved screen, passing behind it on to a wide balcony that overlooked a courtyard. Lucy went with the rest, not certain what to do next. She felt a complete stranger in this place with its alien atmosphere and stiff, formal clothes, and the unsmiling faces and hissing speech placed a further barrier between herself and these people.

Sung Li touched her arm again and said, his voice low, 'The Empress wishes you to see that in China she dispenses justice.'

Lucy glanced inquiringly towards the Empress who, supported by her attendants, glanced back. There was a faint smile on the thin, pale lips, and then there was a clash of cymbals and the loud beating of a gong, and Lucy jumped slightly as marching feet sounded in the courtyard below.

A squad of soldiers, the sunshine glinting on their conical helmets and long spears, had entered the courtyard and now faced the balcony, bowing deeply to the Empress who stood above them. It was some kind of ceremony, Lucy decided and moved nearer to the ledge.

A man was kneeling in the centre of the courtyard, his head bowed and his hands bound behind his back. There was a scarf tied round his eyes and at his side a huge, masked man stood, a sword raised.

It couldn't be happening! She, Lucy Mary O'Malley, could not possibly be standing here, watching a man about to have his head cut off. In a moment she would wake up and find herself in her own small bedroom at Aunt Harriet's house in Oldham.

The Empress flashed her another glance. There was malice in it and an unpleasant flicker of excitement.

'She is waiting for me to scream or faint,' Lucy thought. 'It would please her to see the foreign devil disgrace herself in front of the royal household.'

Something harder and colder than anger rose up in her. She raised her head, clenching her fists, holding her lower lip in her teeth, willing herself to stand motionless. Whatever happened she refused to faint or scream.

The drums rolled again and the Empress raised her arm and let it fall. The blade of the sword sparkled in the sun and something bounced over the ground, streaming scarlet. The courtyard whirled into blackness and a trickle of blood ran from her bitten lip down her chin.

They were all looking at her. She could feel their concerted stare and by an effort of will she had not known she possessed, Lucy turned towards the Empress, folding her shaking hands together and inclining her head. She discerned a gleam of unwilling respect in the snake eyes, and then the Empress turned and made her slow, stately way back to the dragon throne.

Lucy went too, moving on legs that didn't seem to belong to her any more. There were others in the audience chamber now. Men and women in the long robes of the Manchu people, younger people in shorter tunics and trousers, necklaces and bracelets adorning them, their eyes sliding towards her, hands moving to cover their smiles.

'Your husband is come,' the interpreter said at her elbow.

'Husband?' She spoke vaguely, her mind still burdened with horror.

'Prince Chang Lee,' he said, and gave her arm a little shake as if he were rousing her from nightmare, 'In the antechamber.'

He was indicating an arched doorway. Lucy nodded, trying to smile, and went through into a smaller room, furnished with couches. There was the scent of japonica in the air and the walls were hung with peach silk embroidered with threads of white and silver.

'My dear, I have just learned what you were expected to witness,' Chang Lee said, rising and coming towards her. His hands gripped her own and the eyes looking down into hers were warm with indignation.

'An example of the Imperial justice,' Lucy said. She tried to speak lightly, but her voice shook and, to her shame, tears sprang into her eyes and trembled on the tips of her long lashes.

'T'zu Hsi has a cruel streak,' Chang Lee said. 'It amuses her to make fools of people, and she takes a particular pleasure in disgracing any foreigner admitted to the Winter Palace.'

'Oh, hush!' She looked up at him nervously. 'Someone may hear.'

'Then they may have the dubious pleasure of repeating my words to the Empress,' he said, raising his hand and brushing it lightly down her cheek.

There was a tenderness in the gesture that lifted her misery, and she smiled up at him, her eyes kindling with an emotion she was dimly beginning to realise was stronger than anything she had ever felt before.

'You were very brave,' he said, and there was wonderment in his voice.

She had the impression that in a moment, his mouth would press upon hers, and some last barrier would be swept away.

'Prince Chang Lee, good-day to you.'

A young man in European clothes, his fair hair sleeked back, had entered the room with outstretched hand and a smile on his pleasant face.

'Mr Just.' Chang Lee shook hands, turning from Lucy to greet the newcomer.

'And this must be your—fiancée? There were rumours.'

'My bride, Princess Chang Lucy. She and I were wed by proxy.'

'Unusual.' The young man moved towards Lucy and shook hands with her cordially.

His blue eyes were both admiring and puzzled.

'We have mutual acquaintances,' Lucy said. She was so relieved to see a European face that she found herself babbling a little. 'Mr and Mrs Willet, missionaries from Langchow. I travelled with them as far as Tientsin. They asked to be remembered to you if I met you, but I didn't expect it to be here within the Forbidden City.'

'Members of the Diplomatic Corps are occasionally permitted to attend receptions,' he said. 'The Empress dislikes it, but China needs foreign trade so she has to agree to a certain amount of entertaining.'

'The day is coming when China will stand on her own feet without any interference from foreign powers.'

Chang Lee spoke in a cold, hostile voice from which the friendliness had fled.

'Of course there is much that China exports,' Stephen Just said smoothly. 'For my own part I am fascinated by her culture. I find it salutary to remember that when exquisite ivories were being carved here we in Europe were daubing ourselves with woad and running round in skins.'

'My bride has just seen an example of our High Oriental civilisation,' Chang Lee said. 'A local murderer was executed in the courtyard a few minutes ago.'

'I heard something of it. My dear lady, what an appalling affair! I am not surprised you look a trifle pale.'

'It was unpleasant,' Lucy said, and thought how inadequate words were.

'I should think so.' Stephen Just gave Chang Lee a faintly reproachful look.

'My husband was not here, so he was not able to prevent it,' Lucy said quickly.

'Deuced unpleasant though.' He shook his head.

'My wife had an eventful ride from Tientsin,' Chang Lee said. 'The wagon was stopped by Boxers.'

'Good lord!' Now Stephen Just was really startled.

'They wanted payment for a safe journey,' Lucy said. 'We didn't give them anything.'

'Then you were fortunate to get away,' he said solemnly. 'The Boxers have committed some terrible atrocities.'

'The Empress says she is doing everything in her power to check the Boxers,' Chang Lee said. 'One can only hope that she is successful.'

Lucy fancied that she detected a slightly disbelieving look in the young diplomat's eyes, but he tactfully let the comment slip by. Instead he asked politely, 'What part of England are you from? I detect a faint flavour of Lancashire somewhere.'

'More than faint,' she said, amused. 'I was brought up in Oldham by my aunt. My father is Irish though. I haven't seen him for years so Aunt Harriet is really all the family I have.'

'But not the only friends,' he said quickly. 'You must visit the Legation. She is allowed to pass in and out of the city?'

'We are none of us prisoners here,' Chang Lee said, his smile cooler.

'Then we will expect you in a day or two, princess.'

'I shall look forward to it,' she said sincerely.

'If you will excuse us.' Chang Lee bowed. 'I must introduce my bride to some of my own people.'

'I look forward to seeing you at the Legation.' He shook hands again with Lucy.

'Is it far from here?' she inquired as they went back into the throne-room.

'All the legations and embassies cluster like jackals at the gates of the Forbidden City,' he said.

'Didn't you like Mr Just?'

'He's a very amiable young man,' Chang Lee said. 'I notice that he admired you. He could scarcely tear his eyes away.'

'It made a pleasant change,' she said crisply. 'Ever since I arrived in Peking people have been staring at me as if I had two heads or something.'

'It is mainly the red hair,' he said, 'In China it is considered—'

'Unlucky. Yes, I know. Yang Fei told me. I suppose I could dye it black or blonde,' she said.

'The colour of your hair makes no difference to me,' Chang Lee said.

His complete indifference was so palpable that she longed to ask him why he had agreed to the marriage, but some people were coming up and she had to bow and smile as introductions were made.

The vast apartment and the rooms opening out of it were packed with people now. Servants were offering little bowls of sweetmeats and tiny cups of rice wine. In one corner she glimpsed two or three Europeans, looking slightly lost in their dark suits among the brilliant robes and tunics. She would have liked to go and talk to them, but Chang Lee's friends were all around, talking to him while their glances slid round to her. She wished they would speak English and then reproached herself for being unreasonable. After all, if Chang Lee had visited Oldham, none of the people she knew would have been capable of talking Mandarin.

These people evidently knew Chang Lee well. She wondered if they ever remembered that he, too, was not entirely Chinese, that he had been educated in England. His features were slightly broader than theirs, the eyes wider, the cheekbones less pronounced, the skin sallow rather than yellowish. When he smiled his whole face lit up, but he smiled seldom. He seemed to carry a burden of resentment within himself. Perhaps he resented his French blood, wanting to be entirely Chinese. But if that were so, why had he agreed to this marriage with an English girl?

Someone had spoken in English and she started, the words sounding unfamiliar as if they too were foreign.

'I beg your pardon? I'm afraid I was dreaming,' she said hastily.

The man who had spoken to her had

a round face and plump hands covered with rings.

'I ask you, please, if you are happy in the House of the Willow,' he repeated.

'Oh, yes. It's a lovely house,' she said brightly. 'The mandarin has done everything for my comfort.'

'We, too, are very happy that all is settled without harm,' he said.

'Yes, indeed!' She wondered what he meant, but Chang Lee was saying,

'Ching Lo is one of my father's oldest and most esteemed friends.'

'I'm very glad to meet you.' She clasped her hands together and bowed.

'We regret the occurrence you were obliged to witness,' Ching Lo said, lowering his voice. 'There are many beautiful things in China which will please you more, I hope.'

'Very beautiful things. I love the cherry trees and the fruit trees.'

'Ah, you have seen the orchard of Chang Liu,' he said.

'I walked in it.' She felt a blush rising into her cheeks as she realised how close she was to mentioning the pagoda. Hastily she rushed on. 'There's a charming house adjoining it at the other side. I intended to visit, but there was a remarkably fierce dog, a small one, barring the way.'

The smile on Ching Lo's face had frozen as if something had paralysed him. Chatter and laughter flowed all around but she stood in the centre of a little island of silence. She heard her own voice blundering on, shrilly and foolishly.

'You see in England it's customary for near neighbours to call upon one another. I wonder if you know who lives there.'

'It is the house of Mei-Ling,' Ching Lo said. His voice sounded exactly as if he were choking on a fish bone and the smile was clamped to his round face as if it had been fastened there.

'If you will excuse me, I believe I see my father arriving,' Chang Lee said.

His face and voice were expressionless, and he moved away without looking at her. Ching Lo bowed unhappily and they began talking in Chinese again, in the rapid, slightly hysterical manner of people who have just avoided a social disaster.

Her dress of coffee lace with its tight bodice and flounced sleeves, and long, full skirt looked all wrong in these brilliant rooms, among the straight-cut robes of vivid reds and blues. Even her hat, with its wide brim and mass of veiling, looked foolish and fussy. The people here had either short hair or long pigtails skewered into neat buns on top of their heads. She was like a clumsy moth, blundering into a formal and glittering world with no idea of how to survive in it.

Blinking, she turned aside and began to walk slowly down the room, pausing to gaze at the ivories set into niches at intervals along the walls. The ivories were delicately lovely, but they might as well have been railway posters for all the impact they had on her. At the carved screen she paused, sickness sweeping over her. No doubt the courtyard would be empty again now, the blood swilled away, the soldiers with their glistening helmets and spears marched off to guard-duty. Yet she could not have stepped out on that balcony again for a fortune.

'Princess Chang Lucy.'

The voice frightened her, though the interpreter spoke gently and respectfully. She wondered, a little wildly, what new ordeal was prepared for her now.

'The Empress wishes you to accept this, as a marriage gift,' Sung Li said, bowing and offering her a small box.

'Thank you.' She took it and snapped back the lid. Inside, gleaming against dark velvet, was a brooch, its shape that of a tiny dragon fashioned in jade and ruby and lightly speckled with gold. It was a twin miniature of the dragons on the arms of the throne, and even in her present state of mind Lucy could appreciate the beauty of the workmanship.

'You will accept it?' Sung Li's voice was anxious. Lucy wondered if he expected her to fling it on the floor and stamp her foot in temper.

'It's beautiful,' she said, 'I am very grateful to the Empress. Will you tell her so?'

'Certainly, Princess Chang Lucy.' He bowed, relief in his voice.

Lucy took the brooch and pinned it on her dress, above the wide sash. It glittered there, alien against the lace, and she frowned slightly. It ought to have been pinned to the shoulder of a long, straight cut robe such as the others wore. The brooch reminded her that she was a foreigner.

The Empress sat still on her jade throne, but her head was turned slightly towards where Lucy stood. There was no expression on the lined, sagging face but the eyes were brightly inquisitive.

Lucy bit her already sore lip and bowed her head slightly, and the black eyes flicked away again.

'Prince Chang Lee wishes me to tell you that the litter is waiting if you wish to go back to the House of the Willow,' Sung Li said.

So Chang Lee wasn't going to escort her home. Probably his presence was required here. What was certain was that hers was not. Whatever she had said had angered and embarrassed him. Being married she thought, and coming to Peking was like threading a narrow path through quicksand.

'I will go now,' she said.

'I will show you the way to the outer court,' Sung Li said.

It was impossible to tell from his face or voice if he was aware of her mistake. She knew she had made a mistake, but she was still not certain exactly what had been so dreadful about what she had said, and she knew that she would never ask Chang Lee why the house at the other side of the orchard could not be mentioned.

6

'The Empress was pleased with you today,' the mandarin said.

His long fingers were peeling a peach, his eyes downcast. Chang Lee had not joined them for the meal, and no comment had been made on his absence.

'I was not pleased with her, ' Lucy said. 'It was a terrible thing to have to watch.'

'The man was a murderer, and justice must be seen to be done,' he said mildly.

'As an entertainment? They stood and watched as if it were a play!'

'Ah, but you did not lose your face before the court,' he said. 'You displayed a courage and a spirit rare in a foreigner.'

That word again! She was the stranger here and everything she did was judged on that basis. Evidently the mandarin had not been told of her remarks about the house at the other side of the orchard. She wished she did possess the courage and spirit with which he had credited her because then she would have demanded an explanation, but as it was shyness locked her tongue. Shyness and the dread of having Chang Liu's approving manner turn to an icy embarrassment.

'I would like to go into the city in a day or two,' she said. 'It is my aunt's birthday in three months and I wish to send her a present.'

'Which shows a proper respect for your elders.' He looked up nodding, from his peach.

'There is nothing to prevent my going?'

'Nothing at all. I will tell Chin Shu to order a litter,' he began.

'I prefer to walk,' she said swiftly. 'I shall begin to lose the use of my legs soon if I don't get any exercise.'

'Then Chin Shu shall accompany you as guide and interpreter.'

She would have preferred to wander round by herself but no doubt it was more sensible to take someone with her.

The meal was drawing to its close. In the courtyard lanterns flickered about the central fountain and Chen Sula entered and stood silent, hands clasped.

Chang Liu turned and said something in Chinese and the housekeeper answered him. There was pleasure in the tone of her voice, but the words obviously displeased him, for he rose and said, frowningly, in English.

'Please excuse me, Lucy. I have some letters to write.'

'Of course, Chang Liu.' Lucy gave the customary half bow.

Chen Sula lingered, moving to draw a curtain, to move an empty wine glass. It was clear that she had something to say and hoped that Lucy would initiate the conversation.

The girl drank her cooling tea as stolidly as she could. If anyone was going to begin a conversation it would not be herself.

'Prince Chang Lee visits friends this evening,' Chen Sula said at last.

'Oh?' Lucy made the word as non-committal as she could.

'The mandarin wished him to stay at home,' the housekeeper continued.

'Indeed.'

'The prince is often away, visiting friends.'

'Oh.'

It was stupid but she could think of nothing to say but 'oh' and 'indeed.'

'Prince Chang Lee goes his own way in many things.' Chen Sula dusted a few crumbs from the table and slid her gaze towards Lucy. 'You will perhaps find yourself lonely?'

'Heavens, no!' Lucy forced the words out brightly. 'I'm finding everything very interesting indeed.'

'So!' The word had in it a quality of softly malicious amusement.

'I have decided,' Lucy said, taking her courage in both hands and plunging on, 'to have Yang Fei as my personal maid. Perhaps you would tell her?'

'I will consult the mandarin,' Chen Sula said.

'Surely as mistress of the house, I have the right to a maid,' Lucy began.

It was a mistake to let down her guard. Chen Sula gave a tight little smile and said flatly, 'In the house of the mandarin, Chang Liu, there has been no mistress.'

'Since Princess Chang Marie died? Is that what you mean?'

'The Frenchwoman was wife to Chang Liu. She was not mistress here,' Chen Sula said. There was no mistaking the scorn in her voice.

'But surely—?'

'Oh, she was called mistress here,' Chen Sula said. 'The wife of the mandarin is called the mistress, out of custom. I was the one who instructed the servants, and ordered the wine and bought the food. I was the one who arranged for the guests to be entertained!'

So she had been jealous of the French wife the mandarin had brought home. Perhaps it had been a natural emotion, based on distrust of foreigners. Perhaps Chang Marie had not been kind to the servants or had tried to alter the household arrangements.

'I will inform the mandarin that you wish to have Yang Fei as your servant,' Chen Sula said.

The flash of emotion had died, and she spoke formally and flatly.

'One other thing.' Lucy rose, pushing her chair back. It made an ugly sound scraping on the tiled floor.

'Yes?' Chen Sula waited, outwardly respectful, though her eyes were wary.

'The Feast of Ching Ming is over now, isn't it?'

'Yes.'

'Then you needn't trouble to put the yellow chrysanthemums in my room,' Lucy said.

'As you please.' The housekeeper made

no effort to deny that it was she who put them there.

'Thank you. That's all.' Lucy reached for a plum from the silver fruit-bowl on the table, hoping that the other wouldn't notice that her hand was trembling.

Chen Sula bowed and withdrew, treading softly as usual.

If she ate the plum now she would probably squirt the juice down her skirt. Lucy put it back in the dish and went to the windows. One of them was open, but no breeze stirred the curtains. It was very warm, almost stifling even in this large room. She pushed the window wider and stepped over the low step into the courtyard. The moon was rising and it pierced the dark sky like the curve of a bow, diminishing the lantern lights.

She walked across the courtyard and hesitated at the edge of the wood. Seen from a little distance the tips of the trees were hazed with silver but when she stood beneath, the trunks were a ghostly grey and the creepers were black, rustling when she trod near as if they warned her against venturing farther.

She hesitated, shaking her head a little. It was foolish to be nervous. Aunt Harriet had reared her to despise any belief in ghosts or ghouls. Burglars were another matter. Aunt Harriet was certain that after dusk the streets swarmed with husky burglars armed with housebreaking implements. Anything less solid she would have dismissed as silliness.

Lucy could make out the paths twisting ahead. She might have turned back, but something impelled her to walk forward, following the dim track towards the glade. Somewhere a nightjar gave its shrill cry and then there was silence again. She could smell the fragrance of some night-scented blossom and the lichen under her feet had its own spicy aroma. There was, after all, nothing frightening here. The darkness was a cloak and not a threat, and where the path widened into a curve, moonlight lay like pools of silvery water.

She had reached the edge of the glade and the pagoda was a dark bulk, its roof edged with light against its background of trees and sky. Lucy paused and gazed across at it. Within, the crystal lady would be reclining still, her head upon her arm, the piece of carved willow still in her trailing hand. For her this wood had been final refuge. Perhaps she had favoured this spot and come here often, to escape for a short while from the jealousy of Chen Sula, the indifference of the other servants. Lucy could almost see her, flitting through the orchard in her soft, green gown, her fair hair covered by a veil. And when she had reached the little pagoda she had gone inside, into the coolness of stone and mossy floor. The building had looked in daylight, as if it had stood for a long time, built by some Chang ancestor who had also craved a place to dream. Without knowing why she did it, Lucy leaned against the trunk of a tree and sent the name of that other woman fluting softly into the night.

'Chang Marie! Princess Chang Marie.'

There was a whirring of wings as a flock of tiny birds disturbed from their slumber, rose up from their nests. And then, very slowly, the door of the pagoda began to open. The dark bulk was becoming lighter and a figure was emerging, its form clad in long, flowing robes.

For an instant Lucy was convinced that fear had paralysed her. She was rooted to the spot, the little hairs at the back of her neck quivering. For an instant only and then the terror swept through her, galvanising her to action, and she ran back along the twisting path away from the glade. In her mind the figure followed, its footsteps silently gliding over the moss, the wreath of browning blossom on the veiled head. If Lucy turned and waited, the figure would catch up with her, the moonlight glinting on the empty eye sockets, the white bone of the flesh empty face.

Lucy ran harder, her breath pumping in gasps, her hair breaking loose from its pins to tangle on her shoulders. She cannoned into someone and all the strength went out of her limbs so abruptly that she would have fallen had not strong arms held her tightly.

Above her head Chang Lee's voice spoke in astonishment. 'Lucy? Lucy, what on earth's the matter?'

'A ghost—in the pagoda. I saw it!'

'What! Take your time and tell me again.' He held her away from him, shaking her gently, bending his head to see her face.

'In the glade,' she shivered. 'I was there, and I called Chang Marie, and she came. Lee she did! She *did!* The door began to open and then—'

'You called Chang Marie?' he repeated.

'What possessed you to do such a thing?'

'I don't know,' she said. 'I just called, that's all. On impulse. I don't know why. Didn't you ever do anything on the spur of the moment?'

'Yes, but calling up the dead was never a habit of mine,' he said dryly.

'She came, Lee. She did come,' Lucy insisted, shuddering.

'Then we'll go and see, shall we?'

'Back there? Oh, no!' She shook her head, dislodging more pins, and spoke vehemently. 'I'll not go there again tonight!'

'Wait for me here then.' He let her loose and strode off along the path without waiting for an answer.

Her legs were still weak and the perspiration was running down her face. She fumbled for a handkerchief and wiped her damp skin. The wood closed in on her again but somewhere near at hand was the splashing of the fountain.

She was near the courtyard and the big, richly furnished house with its comforting lamps, but she stood motionless, waiting for Chang Lee. In his arms she had felt secure, safe from anything that might injure her.

'There is nobody there,' Chang Lee said, returning.

'Are you sure?' She faced him, anxiously trying to read his expression by the moonlight filtering through the treetops.

'I went inside. There's nothing there except the tomb. The door was ajar but that was probably the wind.'

'There is no wind tonight.'

'The latch is broken. It might have stood so for ages.'

'Were there flowers there?'

'I didn't see any. Why do you ask?'

'Ching Ming,' she said vaguely, not certain how much to reveal of her own visit there.

'We don't keep the feast of Ching Ming in this family,' he said briefly. 'It is my father's wish and I naturally respect it.'

'Were—were your parents not happy together?' she ventured.

'It was a misalliance,' he said shortly. 'It happens in many marriages, and the error is compounded when husband and wife are of different races. Her father was a merchant and my father brought her to the Forbidden City as his bride. She was only sixteen but very lovely.'

'You remember her?' She looked up at

him as they came into the courtyard. He had put his arm around her shoulders and she was beginning to feel close to him again.

'As a kind of dream figure,' he said slowly. 'She hated wearing stiff, formal dresses with bustles and whalebone collars and Chinese fashions didn't suit her, so she devised her own style—very soft and loose with wide sleeves. Always in pastel shades of green and blue. She wore her hair loose too, just held at the side with clips. She could sit on it, that hair. When I was very small I used to trot around after her, holding on to a lock of it. How strange that I should remember that now. I have not spoken about her for years. It would be wiser not to speak of her again.'

Lucy longed to ask why, but feared to spoil the ripening intimacy between them. Instead, as they entered the house, she said.

'I have been thinking that my own dresses look out of place in the Forbidden City. Would it be possible for me to have one or two of the long, straight-cut robes made for me?'

'Yes, of course.' He looked pleased.

'I will tell Chen Sula to inform the dressmaker.'

'No,' she said quickly. 'I am going into the city in a day or two, so I can see a dressmaker there. Chin Shu is to escort me.'

'Good. He's an excellent fellow.'

'And if your father approves I am going to have Yang Fei as my personal maid. She's friendly and can speak some English.'

'By all means. We should have thought of it ourselves.' He crossed to the table, poured two small cups of rice wine, and gave her one.

'It will put some colour back into your face,' he said, as she hesitated. 'You had a bad shock, whatever it was that you saw. Why were you in the orchard?'

She might have asked him the same question, but answered meekly, not wanting to blur the cordiality between them.

'I was too warm indoors, so I wandered out for a breath of air.'

'There has been no rain for weeks,' he said. 'The rice harvest will be sparse if this drought continues. That could mean famine out in the country districts.'

She sipped the wine, remembering the

glimpses of brownish-yellow earth that she had seen on her way to Peking. It seemed wrong that there should be want in this beautiful country. Then she recalled the contrast between the opulence of the throne-room and the bloody scene in the courtyard, and shivered, thinking that China was a land that swung between the extremes of cruelty and loneliness.

'Drink your wine,' Chang Lee said kindly, 'and put the so-called ghost out of your mind. It was a combination of imagination and moonlight.'

'I was thinking of the man who had his head cut off this afternoon,' she told him.

'Forget that too. It won't happen again,' he promised. 'I made my own protest to the Court Chamberlain, reminding him that if word got back to Queen Victoria that one of her female subjects had been constrained to witness such an event relations between our two countries would grow even more strained than they were at present. The Empress is no fool, and she will see the wisdom of that.'

'You're very kind.'

She spoke with sudden embarrassment, aware that, as he talked of the Empress, his eyes rested on her as if he were learning her face. Dark eyes with thick lashes set above broad cheekbones in a face that combined both east and west in a fascinating blend.

'I must look terrible,' she said, putting her hands to her hair. 'My aunt would say that I had been dragged through a hedge backwards!'

'I was thinking that you looked rather charming,' he said, putting down his wine cup and stepping towards her.

'I was not very charming at the Winter Palace,' she said. 'I made you angry and shocked your friends. I'm not certain why, but I am sorry for it. It isn't easy to come as a stranger and not be certain what to talk about, or how to avoid giving offence.'

'I was wrong to be angry.' His voice was sober. 'It was not your fault. You were not to—' He broke off, turning as the door opened and Chen Sula came in.

Lucy could have wept with vexation. She and Chang Lee had actually been talking together as friends talked, and she was certain he had been on the verge of an explanation.

'I beg your pardon,' the housekeeper said in English. 'I thought I heard voices, but I was not aware that you had returned, and I believed Princess Chang Lucy to be in her room.'

'She thought she saw something that frightened her in the orchard,' Chang Lee said.

'Not an intruder! A thief—'

'A ghost.' Chang Lee sounded tolerantly amused. 'She fancied she saw the ghost of my mother, but the moonlight plays tricks. What was it you wanted?'

'Your honoured father asked me to inform him when you came in,' Chen Sula said. 'He is in the library and wishes to speak to you.'

'And he'll be in a bad humour, so I'll not keep him waiting. Goodnight to you, Lucy.'

His voice and manner were still friendly, but whatever had begun to grow between them had been trodden down again. As he went out Lucy caught a gleam of triumph in Chen Sula's black eyes. In sudden, childish pique she said crossly, 'I thought women in China had tiny, narrow feet. Yours are bigger than mine!'

'The Manchus never bind the feet,' Chen Sula said. 'It is a barbaric custom which our government is trying to stamp out. May I close the window now? If there was an intruder—'

'It was my imagination,' Lucy said quickly. 'A trick of the moonlight.'

'They say unquiet spirits build up their shapes out of moonlight and shadow,' Chen Sula said.

'Do they? How foolish of them!' Lucy said lightly. 'Goodnight to you, Chen Sula.'

Without waiting for the other's reply she turned and went out. The lamps made a soft radiance over the main hall and there were tiny bowls of rose petals scenting the air. From behind a nearby door the mandarin's voice rose loudly and angrily and Chang Lee's answered with equal vehemence. They were speaking in Chinese, but it was clear that a furious argument was in progress. As Lucy hesitated the voices died away and she went quickly upstairs, fearing someone might come out and find her standing there.

In her own room she unpinned the dragon brooch and laid it in its velvet-lined case. She was acquiring valuable jewellery, she reflected, and wished that understanding would come to her at the same speed. She would have given a dozen dragons to know what Chang Lee really thought of her. In the space of twenty-four hours he had moved from hostile indifference to polite friendliness, then to cold anger, and thence to a warm cordiality again. As for her own feelings—as she slipped a nightgown over her head, she thought ruefully that she understood her own feelings less than anything. Too much was happening too quickly. It had been a terrible shock to find out she was already married with no opportunity to change her mind, and a worse one to discover that the bridegroom was obviously so reluctant that he had no intention of behaving towards her like a husband.

She sat down before the mirror and began to brush her hair. It glowed like a polished apple and its tendrils curled round her brow in a way that would have been considered very pretty in Europe. Carefully she pulled back the mass of hair slanting her eyes, watching her cheekbones spring into prominence. She looked like a small cat, she decided, and found herself laughing.

Someone had rapped gently on the door. The small noise stifled her laughter, and she let her hair fall free again, waving over her shoulders. Perhaps her instinct had been right and Chang Lee was beginning to admire her.

'Come in.' She raised her voice, anticipation bubbling up in her.

The anticipation died as Chen Sula came in.

'You dropped some hairpins,' she said, bowing as she laid them on the table. 'I feared you might need them.'

'Thank you.' She answered dully, aware of her disappointment.

'So you saw the ghost of the Frenchwoman,' Chen Sula said, lingering.

Lucy had turned to the mirror again but she could see the reflection of the housekeeper, her hands folded within her wide sleeves, her eyes fixed on Lucy's back.

'Oh, I must have imagined it,' Lucy said. 'I am certain that the dead sleep peacefully.'

'If any of them do walk,' Chen Sula said, 'I am certain that the Frenchwoman must do so. Chang Marie would never rest. The wicked never rest.'

'You have no right to say such a thing,' Lucy said. 'No right, at all.'

'I knew her,' Chen Sula said softly. 'I knew her very well. Right from the beginning when the master brought her here, I knew exactly what she was like. I knew it as one woman always knows another one. Oh, she pretended to be friendly. I can see her now, lisping at me in English that was much poorer than my own. "Dear Chen Sula, you must help me to learn Mandarin." She never did learn, of course, and I never bothered to teach her. She took no interest in the master's comfort or the ordering of his household. Idle to the bone, and wanton.'

'Wanton!' Lucy echoed the word in astonishment.

'She was unfaithful,' Chen Sula said.

'I don't believe it,' Lucy said. 'I simply don't believe it.'

'You have seen the carving of the willow tree girl?'

'Yes. Yes, it's very beautiful.'

'A young artist from Shansi came to the Forbidden City, seeking a rich patron. The mandarin sent for him and paid him handsomely to carve the willow-tree girl as a symbol of the family legend. You have heard of the legend?'

'Yes.'

'Lo Kim, that was his name, wished to make a statue of Princess Chang Marie,' the housekeeper said. 'The master agreed. He would have agreed to anything that pleased his wife. She was never happy unless she was getting something. It pleased her vanity to pose for the artist, and it pleased her lust to tease Lo Kim into falling in love with her.'

'I don't want to hear this,' Lucy said faintly, but she was held down to her chair by a terrible fascination. The other was rushing on, as if a dam had burst inside her.

'Better for you to know, lest you mention her name. Her name is not spoken here, and the Feast of Ching Ming is not kept for her. Why should it be? She betrayed my master. He paid her the honour of making her his wife, and she bore him a son. Yet that never satisfied her, never made her happy. Oh, she was a sly one. She used to go off into the orchard, into the glade where the pagoda stands, and she would tell me that the artist must never be disturbed when he was working. Working! I knew what was going on. All the servants knew! Oh, she was clever! The master was blind to her wickedness.

He sorrowed because she was not happy in Peking, and he never guessed, until he found them himself, that she was betraying him, shaming him.'

'He found them?' Lucy's face was white and strained, and her voice was no more than a thread of sound.

'The statue was complete but Lo Kim had stayed on, going every day to the glade, and the Frenchwoman gliding after him, her eyes sly, laughing at us all. The mandarin walked that way by chance, having returned early from the court, and found them embracing. He saw then what she was like, how she had put horns on his head, and shamed the House of Willow. Wives have been killed for less, but even then Chang Liu had mercy. He called the household together in his first anger and dragged her before the servants, telling them to look well at the foreign devil for the last time because he was sending her back to her father, divorcing her and sending her away. Her name was not to be spoken again because it had brought shame and suffering. Oh, that was a terrible day because Chang Liu was so angry, but there was joy in it too, because he was sending her away and he wouldn't have to look at her.'

'But I thought—she died,' Lucy said.

Her lips were dry and she had to swallow painfully before she could articulate the words.

'Oh, yes,' Chen Sula said. Her voice was still soft and there was a dreamy smile on her face as if she were imagining something pleasurable. 'Oh, yes. Princess Chang Marie died, but she'll not rest easily under that statue that was fashioned of her. How could she rest, with her sins to drag her out into the world again, and her last the worst of all. She hanged herself from the willow-tree and so shamed us all.'

7

The next morning it was even warmer than the day before and Lucy felt a trickle of sweat down her back as she dressed. The sky beyond the windows was glittering, metallic blue but there was a hot wind blowing through the gardens, tossing blossom from the trees, bringing with it a thin, reddish dust that lay like fine sand over the courtyard and the steps leading to the terraces.

She had slept badly, her mind constantly struggling to wake her and remind her of the day's events, her body too weary to move. It was no wonder that the name of Chang Marie was never spoken if she had been so blatantly unfaithful to her husband. Part of Lucy's restless mind protested that Chen Sula's jealousy had coloured her account, but such an account could easily be checked at some future time, so she was unlikely to have lied.

Lucy put on her sprigged cotton dress and wound her hair in a thick plait round her head in an effort to remain cool. The day stretched ahead of her, shadowed despite the heat. The tragedy that had happened twenty years before had left its mark upon the family of Chang Liu. It was not surprising that he never visited the pagoda or talked about his dead wife. She wondered if his conscience troubled him when he thought of her suicide, or if he considered his harshness had been justified. Some of the love he felt for her must have remained, else he would surely have destroyed the statue of her and the carving of the Willow tree girl.

Chang Lee had been six at the time of his mother's death. No doubt Chen Sula had taken a delight in telling him how wicked his mother had been. Yet she had not entirely succeeded, for his memories of Chang Marie were gentle ones.

And there *had* been something or someone at the pagoda the previous night! In the light of day she felt able to distinguish between reality and imagination. Someone had answered her call and opened the door. If ghosts did exist she doubted if they had to open doors. It couldn't have been Chang Lee because she had run full tilt into him coming from another direction. Perhaps Chang Liu had slipped out to visit his wife's tomb. Lucy decided there was no point in worrying about it. There were many secrets in this House of the Willow, and she would have to tread cautiously if she were going to make some kind of life here for herself.

When she went downstairs she was met by Chin Shu, who greeted her in his quiet respectful manner and told her that the mandarin and Prince Chang Lee had been summoned to court.

'Do you know why?' she asked, a little fearfully.

'The Empress often sends for her nobles, princess. It is usual,' he said.

'Oh.' She felt faintly cheered, for it had flashed into her mind that the terrible old woman on the dragon throne might very well have taken it into her head to do something dreadful.

'May I bring something for you? It will be late when they return and the days are long,' he said.

'Did Chen Sula tell you that Yang Fei is to be my personal maid?'

'She did say so.'

'Then tell Yang Fei to come to me in the library. I am going to try to learn Mandarin,' she said.

'That will take many years,' he said.

'I intend to be here for many years,' she said firmly.

The library was obviously the room where she had heard Chang Lee and his father arguing. She wondered if they had been arguing about her or if there was some other cause for dissent.

The room was more European in style than the other apartments. Lucy might have been in any English study with its walls of panelled wood, its thick carpets and leather chairs and shelves filled with handsomely bound books. There was a glass-topped case running along one wall filled with scrolls tied with coloured ribbons and cords, but that was the only touch of the Orient she could see.

'Good morning, Princess Chang Lucy,' Yang Fei said politely from the doorway. 'I wish, please, to thank you for the honour you pay me. I was not trained to be personal servant, so you will kindly excuse me if I make mistakes.'

'I was not trained to have a personal maid,' Lucy said frankly, 'so I probably won't notice any mistakes. Close the door and come and sit down. I want to learn some simple phrases in Mandarin. We will do this every morning until I begin to understand.'

Yang Fei looked slightly alarmed at the prospect of instructing her new mistress but she did as she was bade, her shyness diminishing into giggles as the morning wore on and Lucy tangled her tongue in the odd clicks and hisses that seemed to comprise even the simplest Chinese sentence.

'Chin Shu was right,' she said at last.

'It will take me many years to learn!'

'Best to haste slowly in Chinese saying,' Yang Fei told her.

'It's an English saying too,' Lucy said, smiling.

The full booming of the gong came from the hall.

'Time for eating, princess.' Yang Fei rose and stood, hands clasped, waiting for orders.

'Then I shall go and eat. Thank you for helping me. We'll get on with the lessons tomorrow.'

'Thank you.' Yang Fei bowed and opened the door.

'Who lives in the house at the other side of the wood?' Lucy asked.

She noticed with interest that Yang Fei had stopped dead.

'You mean—' The girl hesitated, her eyes lowered.

'Simply give me the name of the person who lives there,' Lucy said patiently.

'It is Mei-Ling,' Yang Fei said. Her voice was reluctant, and she wouldn't meet Lucy's eyes.

Lucy wanted to know who Mei-Ling was, but before she could frame a question the maidservant had whisked away.

A meal had been set in the elegant dining-room, but there was no sign of Chen Sula or Chin Shu. Instead, one of the other servants waited on her, and it was clear from his uneasy manner and the distance he kept between them when he was handling the dishes that he was not happy to be serving a foreign devil.

After the meal she went up to her room again. The bed had been made, the breakfast tray removed and her discarded garments hung up. There were fresh towels in the bathroom, even a new cake of soap in the copper dish.

The household ran as smoothly as if it had been oiled, and it made no difference if she were there or not. At Aunt Harriet's she had had responsibilities to give shape and meaning to her days.

Impatiently she thrust away the mood of despondency that threatened to descend on her, and went to the wardrobe to pick out a dress that was suitable to wear for an afternoon visit.

The cotton dresses were too informal, the green wool too warm, the evening gown too low-necked for the daytime. In the end she put on her coffee lace again, tying the ribbons of the wide hat, drawing on the long gloves. Whatever her private nervousness she looked cool and elegant. Taking up her cream parasol, Lucy hesitated, and then stepped out to the balcony. With any luck she would be able to visit the house at the other side of the orchard and return before anyone missed her.

It was not a day for walking. The hot, dry wind still blew, and as she passed the fountain she noticed a film of reddish dust mingling with the water and dulling the little coloured stones. The trees were shedding fragments of blossom, showering her with confetti. It was a pity she didn't feel more like a bride, she thought ruefully, ducking to avoid an errant branch.

She went through the glade with only a swift glance at the pagoda. That could wait for another day. That afternoon she was determined to find out why Mei-Ling's house was not to be mentioned in conversation.

She had reached the long flight of steps leading to the courtyard, and for a moment she paused, bracing herself for the possible onslaught of a savage, lion-maned dog. There was no sound however and the shutters hung flat behind the narrow windows. If she turned now and went back nobody would ever know that she had been there.

Lucy set her foot on the lowest step, drew a deep breath, and went on up. The high, wrought-iron gate opened noiselessly and she went round the corner of the building and hesitated outside another high gate which shielded a deep porch.

This was clearly the front of the house. The windows were closely shuttered; the porch led to a lacquered red door; there was a secretive look about the place that contrasted with the charming garden behind her. The only sound was the tinkling of the bells swinging wildly in the wind. Lucy noticed the big bell hanging by the gate and pulled its thick rope before she had more time to reconsider.

Within the house sounded the furious barking of a dog. Instinctively she took a firmer grip of her parasol, bent on using it to protect herself if any fury of fur launched itself at her.

The red door opened and an elderly Chinaman, his hair in a long pigtail, shuffled to the other side of the gate. His eyes were raised to hers with a questioning look, and she said, her voice as slow and clear as she could make it.

'Princess Chang Lucy to see Mei-Ling.'

The old man turned and shuffled away without answering, closing the door behind him. The barking of the dog died away and, save for the tinkling of the bells, there were several moments of silence.

Lucy had begun to contemplate pulling the main bell rope again when the door was opened and the servant reappeared, coming up to the gate and drawing it back.

'Please. Come.' He stood aside to allow her to pass him, and she heard the gate clang shut as she went through the inner door to a wide, yellow-painted hall with a staircase twisting up out of it.

'This way, please.' The old man led the way across the hall and down a narrow passage to a curtained arch. He held the curtain aside and Lucy found herself in a small apartment, its walls hung with pale yellow. Its windows shuttered. The light filtering through the slats revealed two or three bamboo chairs and a low table. There was a vase on a shelf against the wall with one magnificent spray of red-hearted lilies in it, but apart from that the room was without ornament.

The old man pulled up one of the blinds, flooding the room with sunshine, and went through another archway at the other side. The room looked out upon the garden but Lucy had time for only a brief glance before the patter of feet from beyond the arch heralded the arrival of a young Chinese woman. Young and very beautiful, the girl thought, staring at the tiny, exquisitely clad figure. A robe of a deeper yellow than the walls covered her from neck to toe, its hem embroidered with tiny black pearls that glinted when the sunlight caught her. Her blue-black hair was coiled in a thick plait on top of her small head and her face was painted, the long eyelids brushed with blue shadow, the mouth rosier than nature had intended. At the young woman's side was the dog that had frightened Lucy away before. It was not barking now but it growled, deep in its throat, as she took a pace forward.

'Princess Chang Lang?' The other bowed, a smile on the full pink mouth. 'I apologise for delay, but you did not warn of your coming.'

'I know. I'm sorry, but in my country near neighbours often call without giving any notice,' Lucy said, a trifle flustered, as she bowed with one eye on the growling dog.

'Few visit the house of Mei-Ling,' the other said.

'Are you—?'

'I am Lady Tong Mei-Ling,' the young woman informed her. 'Please to sit. The dog will not attack unless I order.'

'Oh; Good!' Lucy sat down on one of the bamboo chairs.

'You will take tea? I have told the servant to bring some.'

'Yes, thank you. I was—was just walking in the orchard, and I was nearby so thought I'd drop in.'

'Drop in?'

'Call. Call upon you.'

'Excuse, please. My English is not yet perfect,' Mei-Ling said, taking one of the other chairs.

'It's a lot better than my Chinese,' Lucy said ruefully.

'You are learning our tongue?' Mei-Ling raised winged black brows.

'As I am now living here it seemed the sensible thing to do,' Lucy said.

'And the English are most sensible people,' Mei-Ling said. 'My mother told me that you had come.'

'Your mother?'

'Madam Tong Chen Sula is my mother,' Mei-Ling said calmly. 'Here is the tea.'

The servant had returned with a tray on which teacups of an almost transparent delicacy were set. Lucy took her own without realising exactly what she was doing. Her eyes were still fixed on Mei-Ling, who smiled gently as she sipped the steaming liquid.

'Your mother is Chen Sula?' Lucy said at last.

'She did not tell you? I am a person of small importance,' Mei-Ling said, ducking her head with the smile still on her lips.

'I didn't know that Chen Sula had ever been married,' Lucy said, and promptly blushed scarlet. It was possible that Chen Sula never had been married.

'My father was Tong Chen,' Mei-Ling said. 'He died when I was ten years old.'

'And this was his house?'

'A humble one,' said Mei-Ling. 'My father was steward to the mandarin, Chang Liu. Much respected.'

So then Chen Sula had been married and widowed herself, and had borne a daughter. Lucy wondered if this marriage had been a happy one, and doubted it.

'Chen Sula didn't tell me,' she repeated stupidly.

'In China we do not speak much of our families to—foreigners,' Mei-Ling said.

That word again! Lucy drank her tea too quickly and choked slightly.

'You were walking in the wood?' her hostess said after a moment. Her tone conveyed a hint of disbelief.

'It's a beautiful place,' Lucy said.

'Much of Peking is beautiful,' Mei-Ling said.

'Indeed it is!' Lucy answered eagerly, relieved that the conversation had turned into a safer channel. 'I went to the reception at the Winter Palace, and I was very impressed by the splendour all round me.'

'And the Empress? What do you think of the Empress?' Lucy hesitated. She had already learned that in this country it was foolish to speak without thought.

'She is a remarkable woman,' she said at last.

'She is the most popular woman in China,' Mei-Ling said, lowering her voice. 'One word from her and off comes your head!'

'Not without trial, surely?' Lucy said.

'Oh, there is a trial very often,' Mei-Ling said, shrugging her shoulders. 'But the word of the Empress is the law in the Forbidden City. It is not wise to offend her. Will you have more tea, Princess Chang Lucy?'

'Thank you, no.' Lucy put her cup on one of the small tables and the dog growled again, its eyes following the movement of her hand.

'Ming is not used to strangers,' Mei-Ling said, 'but he will not bite until I tell him to bite. Then he will hang on until I tell him to stop. He barked at you when you came the other time.'

'And you watched me from the window,' Lucy said.

'I was—curious,' Mei-Ling said, 'as you were curious. You ought to have entered.'

'The dog startled me,' Lucy said, 'but now that we have introduced ourselves there is nothing surely to prevent our visiting each other?'

'It would not be fitting,' Mei-Ling said.

'Because you are Chen Sula's daughter? I don't see what that could possibly have to do with it.'

'Nothing,' Mei-Ling said. 'It has nothing to do with it. Come! I will show you my garden. It would be best if you did not speak of your visit here.'

'Why?' Forgetting her determination to be tactful, Lucy spoke bluntly. 'What is so terrible about my visiting you?'

'It would be against custom,' Mei-Ling said, rising and smoothing the skirt of her robe with her narrow hands. On one finger glinted the huge diamond that Lucy had seen before.

She would have pursued the question but the other had moved to the door and she was constrained to follow. The servant, bowing as he shuffled forward, opened the door and the gate, and the two young women stepped out into the garden, Mei-Ling drawing a yellow scarf over her high-piled hair.

The wind was still boisterous, whipping at the hem of Lucy's dress and the wide brim of her hat.

'Come,' Mei-Ling said again. 'My garden is small and not worthy of your admiration, but others have had the kindness to say it has merit.'

It was as small and exquisite as herself, its paths lined with tiny shells, a dolphin of milky jade spouting water into a shallow basin, the green of bamboo contrasting with a bush of white japonica. In the angle between two walls a tiny summerhouse, its pagoda roof edged with copper, provided shelter from the wind.

'It is most pleasant to sit here,' Mei-Ling said. Her eyes roamed slowly over Lucy's slightly dishevelled frame with a look that made the other wonder if she had deliberately brought her out into the wind.

'You will see that from this place one may see the entire garden and the steps too. That is the way that visitors usually come.'

Instead of through the orchard and up the steps to the back, Lucy thought, I take the point.

Aloud she said. 'Your garden is most restful.'

'Not always. My son can be most noisy,' Mei-Ling said, bending to pick up something from the path ahead. It was a little carved horse painted red and blue. 'He leaves his toys, you see.'

'Your son?'

'Tong Su,' the other said. 'He is only three years old, so I do not scold.'

The child who had run off when she had seen him in the courtyard of the mandarin's house! It had been the same child who had flashed through the wood and whom she had followed to this house.

'Children can be very wearisome,' Mei-Ling said. 'You will find it too, one day when you have had a child of your own.'

'I didn't know you were married,' Lucy said.

'Married?' Mei-Ling dropped her eyes, the smile on her lips broadening. 'Oh, I am not married, Princess Chang Lucy. I have never been married.'

Lucy stood on the shell-edged path, her gaze riveted to the colourful little horse, and felt sure as if a gulf had suddenly yawned at her feet. The child was the reason why the name of Mei-Ling had embarrassed Yang Fei so much when she had been forced to speak it. The child was the reason that everybody had fallen silent when she had mentioned the neighbouring house.

She wanted to ask the question that blazed in her mind, but her mouth was dry, her lips chapped by the wind. Bits of sand blew into her eyes, stinging them.

'My son is not at home today,' Mei-Ling said, 'or you might have seen him. He is much like his father, so those who have seen him say.'

Her smile mocked and her eyes were lit with hidden laughter.

'If you will excuse me, I ought to be going,' Lucy heard herself say, her voice sounded harsh and unreal in her own ears.

'Will you drink more tea before you leave?' Mei-Ling asked, putting down the horse and slanting a questioning glance up at the taller girl.

'Thank you, no.'

'It was most gracious of you to visit me,' Mei-Ling said. 'We will not speak of the visit to others, for it is against custom.'

Against custom for a wife and a mistress to drink tea together. It was all becoming clear now. Chang Lee's resentment at the marriage into which he had been forced, the argument between himself and his father the previous evening—the 'friends' he had gone out to visit must have been Mei-Ling and his little son. No wonder there had been a frozen silence when she had artlessly inquired who lived in the house at the other side of the orchard! And it was no wonder either that Chen Sula disliked her so much. In the housekeeper's eyes she was the hated foreigner who had come to supplant her daughter in Chang Lee's affections just as the Frenchwoman had come to cheat Chen Sula out of her own hopes of marrying the mandarin.

Mei-Ling was bowing and Lucy must have made some gesture in return because she was hurrying through the gate again and round the side of the house to the second gate and so down the steps. The wind blew more fiercely, parching her throat, and the wind bells jangled in her ears. If she looked back she would see Mei-Ling watching her leave, see the gently mocking smile on the carefully painted face and the yellow maned dog crouched at her side, waiting for the order to spring.

She didn't look back but hurried down into the wood, her head lowered into the wind. The glade was a mass of fallen blossom, and the pagoda was whirling with tinkling bells.

Chang Marie. Chang Lucy. They were linked already by the repetition of an old tragedy played out on an old stage with new actors to play the roles. Lucy turned abruptly and ran across to the pagoda, pushing open the door. Her feet sank into the grey lichen and the thick walls banished the scorching wind. She closed the door and stood with her back against it, the dimness soothing her eyes, her breath coming in great gulps. From the alcove where the lady of crystal lay a figure in long robes rose and bowed.

8

Lucy had never been so terrified in her life. Her legs shook so violently that she could not even have run, but leaned weakly against the closed door, her eyes fixed on the figure as it approached.

'Only fools faint,' was one of Aunt Harriet's well-worn sayings.

Lucy, promising herself crazily that she wouldn't be a fool, forced herself to stand upright, shaking her head dizzily.

'You are sick, lady?'

The voice was a man's voice and the face, staring down at her own, was that of an elderly Chinaman.

'You startled me,' she said through dry lips, 'I thought you were Chang Marie!'

'You are the lady who called here last

night,' he said slowly.

'And you opened the door and came into the glade!'

'There was nobody there,' he said. 'I began to think it was the spirit of Chang Marie calling her own name.'

'And I began to think she had answered to my call,' Lucy said and laughed shakily.

'The moonlight robs us of our wits,' he said. 'Will you not sit a moment to recover from your fright?'

There was nothing to sit on but a moss-grown log. Lucy lowered herself to it gingerly and the man took his place at the other end, folding his long robe about him. On his pigtailed head was a small cap and his long hands were decorated with rings.

'I am Lucy,' she said. 'Princess Chang Lucy.'

'Lo Kim,' he said.

She suppressed a violent start. So this was Chang Marie's lover, the artist who had seduced her when he sculpted her and been the cause of her suicide.

'Ought you to be here?' she ventured.

'You have heard of me?' He glanced at her sharply.

'You carved the statue and the one in

the house,' she said.

'My two finest works,' he said without conceit. 'I have done nothing comparable since.'

'Do you live in the Forbidden City?' she asked in surprise.

'Beyond the walls. My house is near the Ha Ta gate. Oh, it is only since I returned from my travels. I went to the high country that lies between us and India to study and pray and perfect my art. I spent ten years in the monasteries of Tibet, seeking the Tao.'

'The Tao! What's that?'

'Tao is the way,' he said. 'Once you have found it you have only to follow it to the end, but there are those who never find it.'

She wondered if he had but didn't like to ask him. Instead she said, her voice overbright in the gloom of the pagoda, 'You speak English perfectly.'

'Thank you for your kind words. My knowledge of your language improved greatly during my sojourn in Tibet,' he said smiling. 'One of the monks there was an Englishman. He also was seeking the Tao, but he took the trouble to spend many hours instructing me.'

'And then you came back to Peking?' She looked at him questioningly, too shy to ask further what she really wanted to know but hoping that he would confide in her.

'But I live outside the gates,' he said. There is too much corruption within the walls. I prefer to walk freely.'

'You come here,' she pointed out.

'There is a small gate in the orchard wall,' he said. 'At the time of Ching Ming I come to pay my respects to the poor lady.'

'She killed herself,' Lucy accused.

'Poor soul.' His voice was sad, but curiously impersonal as if Chang Marie had been nothing more to him than the model for his art. 'She was a most unhappy lady. Most homesick for France. She had been born and lived there until she went with her father to Indo-China. Then she came to Peking to the Forbidden City.'

'As the wife of the mandarin. I know.'

'You have been talking to Chen Sula,' he said, a wry smile on his face. 'She never liked me.'

'Perhaps she had cause,' Lucy said.

'She has been talking to you, then?'

'A little.'

'And no doubt she told you that I had been Chang Marie's lover?'

'Yes. Yes, she did.' Lucy, feeling suddenly embarrassed, said awkwardly. 'It's none of my business.

'But if you are wed to Chang Lee, then you are part of the family.'

'You know who I am, then?' she frowned.

'It is known in the city that the son of the mandarin, Chang Liu, has married an Englishwoman. I saw you here before when I brought the wreath for Chang Marie, and later I found the vase of flowers. You had put them here, I think.'

'You were going to speak of Chang Marie,' she reminded him.

'There is not much to tell,' Lo Kim said. 'I was a young man, an artist without a patron. I came to Peking, hoping to make my reputation here, and Chang Liu employed me to carve the figure of the girl in the willow tree. He was pleased with the work and asked me to stay on in order to carve a figure of his wife. She was a most beautiful lady and a most unhappy one. Chen Sula was not a help. She did not try to make Chang Marie feel welcome. It is my belief that she hoped to wed

Chang Liu herself, but he saw her only as a servant and arranged for her marriage to his steward.

'And Chang Marie?'

'She was unhappy,' he repeated. 'There was nothing for her to do in Peking, and she was seldom invited to court because the Empress was not pleased that Chang Liu had married a foreigner. We became friends, she and I. There were long hours when I would work on my carving and she would lie, very still, and talk to me of her home and her father. I fell in love with her. I think now that I loved most the beauty in her that spurred my hand to carve work such as I have never done before and will never do again.'

'You were lovers,' Lucy said in bewilderment.

'No. No, we were never lovers,' he said. 'I did not feel for her in that way. One cannot love a statue, an idea, a flower. The statue was finished, ready to be placed in the hall of the mandarin's house where visitors could admire it. She came into the orchard to thank me privately. She told me she would be more unhappy than ever when I had gone, that Chang Liu neglected her and that the servants thought of her still as a foreign devil. I put my arms about her, as a friend might do. Perhaps more might have followed, but Chang Liu came upon us. He would not listen to us when we tried to explain but ordered me to leave before he had me killed. I am an artist, not a brave man, and so I left.'

'And Chang Marie hanged herself,' Lucy whispered.

'According to our customs she brought double shame to her husband,' he nodded. 'I came back when I heard what had happened. I tried to tell Chang Liu, but he did not know by then what to believe, and Chen Sula was at his elbow, whispering poison into his ear. He told me to go away, never to trouble him again, but he put my statue here in the place where he had laid her. I have not done such fine work since.'

'But you come here, even when the Feast of Ching Ming is over.'

'To look at my work,' he said, 'I am the only one who looks at it now. I come through the little gate. It does no harm and it feeds an old man's vanity. I shall owe you an inestimable favour if you do not speak of my coming.'

Soon she would have as many secrets as

anyone else to keep, Lucy thought.

'Do you know Tong Mei-Ling?' she asked.

'The daughter of Chen Sula? She was a tiny child when I left. Now she lives—'

'I know where she lives. Have you seen her since you returned to Peking?'

He shook his head.

'I seldom leave my house except to come here,' Lo Kim said. 'I came back to find my father had died a comparatively rich man, so I do not need to earn my bread, I do not even need to paint or carve. That spark died with Chang Marie.'

'I see.' Lucy spoke slowly, her eyes on the gleaming figure in the alcove. The history of Chang Marie was more tragic than she had guessed, for it was a history of misunderstanding and waste.

'You will not tell?' Lo Kim said anxiously, seeing her rise.

'I'll not tell.' She hesitated, then put out her hand in the European fashion. 'I hope that you find the—Tao.'

He clasped her fingers briefly and moved away. She glanced back as she opened the door, but he was gazing at his masterpiece again.

In some obscure fashion her encounter

with Lo Kim had both soothed and saddened her. Chang Liu had refused to listen to his wife's explanation and two lives had been wasted because of it—perhaps three, for Chang Liu's conscience must surely have troubled him sorely. Certainly he had never taken another wife.

As she made her way back to the house, Lucy vowed that she would not rush into accusations, but would wait patiently. If she and Chang Lee could become true friends, then he might confide in her about Mei-Ling and her child of his own accord. Friendship would be a start, at least, and could lead—to what? She felt the colour rise in her face again and it was not caused by the heat of the wind.

To her relief she didn't appear to have been missed and, changing back into her sprigged cotton, she went down to the library where she occupied herself in writing a long letter to Aunt Harriet. It would do no good to worry her aunt, with talk of the Boxers or of Chang Lee's neglect of her. Instead she mentioned briefly that she was already married and then launched into a long description of the beauty of the house and the magnificence of her reception at court. That would please Aunt Harriet, who could read it to the Vicar. Nowhere in the letter did she mention the sad history of Chang Marie or hint at the existence of Mei-Ling and her son.

She had just sealed the letter when Chang Lee came in. He wore the short tunic and the trousers affected by younger members of the court; these were of dark red silk faced with gold and above the high collar his face was sombre.

For a moment Lucy feared that he had heard of her visit to Mei-Ling, but his first words reassured her.

'I leave you too much alone, but the Empress called a full Council and I have been delayed there until now. My father is not yet returned.'

'Is something wrong?' she asked.

'There are reports of a British ship being fired on at Tientsin,' he said. 'The ambassador is demanding an explanation and threatening to sue for damages. The Empress declares she cannot be held responsible for the actions of an illegal organisation.'

'The Boxers?'

'They grow in strength and ferocity,' he said. 'Oh, their aims are not discreditable. They wish to rid China of foreign corruption but their methods are ferocious. I cannot condone terror and murder as instruments of reform.'

'Does the Empress?' Lucy asked.

'Who knows what T'zu Hsi really thinks?' He spread his hands wide. 'She is a riddle even to herself, I suspect. Her nephews, Prince Tuan and Prince Su, have tried to persuade her to speak clearly, but she will do nothing.'

'We had a queen like that once,' Lucy said, remembering her history lessons. 'Queen Elizabeth had a treaty with Spain, but she secretly encouraged her sea-captains to attack and rob Spanish treasure ships.'

'This is 1900, not the sixteenth century.'

'Exactly!' she said, with a flash of spirit. 'The world is growing smaller and countries ought to draw nearer together in friendship!'

'Europe has exploited all the resources of China,' he said, 'and given little back. Oh, I know the missionaries try to help the poor but it's at the expense of our own ancient faith. Do you know what year this is?'

'1900,' she said in surprise.

'In our reckoning it is the Year of the Rat,' Chang Lee said. 'A year of change and turmoil. The Lord Buddha called the animals before him, so the legend goes, and twelve of them came, so to each one he gave a year. The rat was the first to obey his call so when the Year of the Rat comes it is a time of new and violent beginnings.'

'What year were you born in?' she asked, fasinated by this novel way of reckoning time.

'The Year of the Cock,' he said, smiling at her, 'Cock people are reputed to be adventurous, pioneering, boastful and amorous.'

'And what am I? I am eighteen.'

'I did inquire your age before I agreed to the marriage,' he said. 'You are a Snake lady.'

'How horrid!'

'Not at all,' he said teasingly. 'Snake people have magnetic charm, and a great capacity for devotion. Their great fault is their obstinacy.'

'Aunt Harriet would agree with you,' Lucy said.

'And snakes and cocks are said to make excellent marriage partners.' He had taken a seat opposite her and, though the mischievous grin lingered on his mouth, his eyes were kind. 'I fear we made a bad beginning. It was insensitive of me to fail to realise that a girl likes to have a real wedding with a pretty gown and flowers strewn before her.'

How like a man to think that it was only the actual ceremony that bothered her! She gave him an exasperated look and said bluntly.

'It is not the wedding that matters but the marriage!'

'And ours is not yet a true marriage.' He gave her an equally candid look.

'I know this marriage was not to your liking,' she said, twisting her fingers together. 'The Empress ordered it and everyone has to obey the Empress. I know that too. At least I went into it of my own free will.'

'And met with a poor welcome.' He rose and walked over to the window, his back towards her. 'I would ask you to be patient,' he said. 'I have various matters to settle before I come to you as a husband. You must not imagine that I dislike you. I find you—quite charming.'

'For a European?' she finished wryly.

'I am half-European myself,' he said sombrely. 'I know what it's like to have one foot in one world and one foot in another world, for I have travelled in both and never been fully part of either.'

'Your mother—,' she began, but he turned, frowning.

'My mother was a lovely lady and, I believe, a maligned one. Even my father begins to believe that her behaviour was unwise rather than wicked. Chinese women don't act with such reckless friendliness towards other men, but my father never took that into account.'

'And European men don't marry young women they have never seen and keep a mistress at the bottom of the garden,' Lucy thought.

Aloud, she said placatingly, 'I have begun to learn Mandarin. Yang Fei is teaching me but I'm afraid I shall take years to learn it properly.'

'The sounds are very different for a European to pronounce,' he said. 'It is to your credit that you begin to study at all. Most of the English people at the Legation imagine they will be understood by the most ignorant coolie if they speak English very loudly!'

'Stephen Just didn't seem like that,' she objected.

'No, he's a good fellow,' Chang Lee said carelessly. 'You must pay a courtesy call at the Legation soon. It will be pleasant for you to mingle with your own countrymen.'

'I live in Peking now,' she said, drawing a deep breath and rising to face him. 'When I came here I came prepared to marry a Chinese husband and to live as the Chinese do. I don't believe in looking back, but you must give me a little time to—to grow accustomed to all the newness around me.'

'My dear.' He stepped towards her, cupping her face in his hands. 'My dear Lucy, I am ashamed to have neglected you so greatly when you are ready to go to such trouble to please me. We must spend more time together, learn to be friends.'

In a moment he would kiss her. She could already feel, in imagination, his mouth pressing her lips into happy surrender. Her flesh tingled and a slow warmth invaded her loins, twisting upward.

'Princess Chang Lucy,' Chen Sula said from the doorway.

'What is it?' He spoke in English his long fingers laid against Lucy's face still.

Chen Sula spoke rapidly in Chinese, and

he dropped his hands, striding past her to where the housekeeper stood, addressing her in the same tongue in a sharp questioning tone.

'What is it? Has something happened?' Lucy asked.

'I have to go out again,' he said. 'A small matter of business to attend. I will be as speedy as I can.'

He was gone before she could question further and, a few seconds later she glimpsed his tall figure hurrying through the courtyard towards the orchard. Without stopping to think Lucy said. 'He has gone to the house of Mei-Ling!'

At least her incaution had startled the housekeeper. Chen Sula's mouth dropped open foolishly and her tone was alarmed as she said.

'You know about Mei-Ling?'

'I know she is your daughter and the child, Tong Su, her son. You didn't think I would be ignorant for ever, did you?'

'I will have Yang Fei beaten,' Chen Sula said flatly.

'Yang Fei didn't tell me. None of the servants did. It was Mei-Ling herself when I visited her.'

'The mandarin gave orders that you were

not to be told,' the housekeeper said. 'He did not wish his son's bride to lose face.'

'Then the mandarin is a fool. I lose more face, as you call it, when I am kept in ignorance of what everybody else knows,' Lucy said stormily. 'All this fuss and bother because my husband had a mistress and fathered a child! The same thing happens in England too sometimes, and then the man falls in love with a respectable girl and marries her and—'

'In love?' Chen Sula's arched brows climbed towards her hair line. 'You do not fancy Prince Chang Lee loves you, do you. The marriage was arranged by order of the Empress.'

'He is beginning to like me,' Lucy said. She hated being dragged into this argument but Chen Sula's mocking voice spurred her on.

'Like? Oh, that is possible,' the other said. 'Chang Lee has the blood of a foreign devil in himself, but I reared him to be Chinese. Even after his father sent him to school and to the university in Europe, he chose to return here. He returned to the Forbidden City!'

'And Mei-Ling was here.' Lucy's voice was almost inaudible, but the other caught her up on her words.

'Mei-Ling was here and very beautiful. If you visited her, then you will know how beautiful she is. She was seventeen when Chang Lee returned and I knew, as soon as he laid eyes on her that he desired her. Oh, I said nothing, but I watched and waited. He took her to court with him and people admired her. She behaves like a great lady, not like the daughter of a servant. Mind, though her father was only a steward, there is good blood in our family. I had every hope they would wed, if the mandarin could be induced to give his consent.'

It would have delighted her, Lucy thought, if, having failed to snare the mandarin herself, she had succeeded in wedding her daughter to Chang Liu's son.

'They didn't marry,' she said.

'Because Prince Tuan saw my daughter when she went to court,' Chen Sula said. 'He is the most powerful person in China, next to the Empress herself, and it was not wise to oppose him. He wished to make Mei-Ling one of his concubines. There are dozens of royal concubines, quarrelling and plotting behind closed doors with eunuchs to guard them. Chang Liu wished her to accept the offer. I knew then that he thought of her still as a servant's daughter, fortunate to enter a harem but not good enough to marry his precious son!'

'I'm sorry,' Lucy said inadequately. She wished that she could feel more sympathy, but the spitefulness in Chen Sula's face precluded it.

'Chang Lee defied the Empress!' she said now, lifting her head proudly. 'He and Mei-Ling together, swearing they would marry in spite of anything she ordered. Oh, they were brave words, but they were empty ones! Nobody could marry in the Forbidden City without T'zu Hsi knowing about it, and nobody would perform the ceremony without her knowledge.'

'Chang Lee married me,' Lucy said. 'Whatever happened before he agreed to marry *me!*'

'Better marry a foreign devil than lose one's head,' Chen Sula said.

'Lose one's—what are you *talking* about?' Lucy demanded.

'The Empress is not pleased when one of her courtiers defies her,' said Chen Sula. 'Chang Lee had caused the royal household a loss of face and that was something T'zu Hsi could not forgive. She brooded upon it, waiting for the chance to shame the family of Chang Liu. She found the perfect way when he and some of the city merchants asked her permission to travel into England. She told Chang Liu that she would keep his son hostage until his return, and that he must bring back a wife for Chang Lee. A foreign devil with red hair, the Empress said. It did not matter who the girl was, the Empress said. Chang Liu had wed a foreign devil himself and ought not to mind his son bedding one. And she swore that if the mandarin failed in his task then his son would be executed.'

It was clear now why Chang Liu had sought her for a bride for his son. Even her red hair had been a part of it. Yet she was impelled to protest.

'The Empress has no right. I was never even told!'

'You agreed to wed the mandarin's son,' Chen Sula said, shrugging her shoulders. 'We were bidden never to speak of the matter to you, but most people know how it is between Mei-Ling and Chang Lee, and pity him for being forced into marriage with a foreign devil.'

'You cannot know how Chang Lee feels,' Lucy said. 'Not now!' Chen Sula laughed briefly. 'I reared the prince, even before his mother died. I was his nurse and I took care of him. The Frenchwoman had no real interest in him, just as she had none in his father. Always gazing at herself in mirrors as if she were the most beautiful creature in the world! I was the one who cared for the child, and he and Mei-Ling were much of an age. He was only four when she was born, you know, and he told me she was like a little flower. They were always together when they were children, hand in hand.'

'He was not married to me then,' Lucy said.

'You think he considers himself married to you!' The housekeeper laughed again and the sound was not a pleasant one. 'You, with your pink face and your red hair and your dresses with the necks so low a Chinese girl would be ashamed to wear them! I tell you Chang Lee will never come to your bed. Why should he, when Mei-Ling lives so near?'

'The mandarin—,' Lucy choked.

'The mandarin cannot prevent his son from seeking his pleasure where he will.

Oh, he will be kind to you because you are far from home and he has a kindly nature, but when Mei-Ling whistles he will go running to her. And what will you do then? Will you complain to the Empress? Do so and she will only laugh at you. Once she shamed this family by forcing the marriage upon Chang Lee she cared nothing for what happened afterwards.'

Lucy could no longer endure the gibing voice and the glittering eyes of the plump woman who faced her. She pushed past blindly into the hall, but the voice followed her.

'He has gone to her now as you guessed. Tong Su has fallen and grazed his knee. It was not a serious accident, but he went at once. He did not wait to explain to you. He did not even look at you when he left. It is Mei-Ling who sent for him and he went.'

Lucy put her fingers in her ears and ran up the stairs and down the passage to her room, stumbling over the hem of her dress as she went. It was foolish and she would regret it later, but at that moment she would have done anything in the world to find herself back in Oldham, getting ready to go to work in Sawyer's Mill. She had made the most terrible mistake of her life when she had agreed to marry an unknown man and travel out to this unknown land. Chang Lee had been forced to the marriage by a vengeful Empress who chopped off heads as easily as if they were cabbages, but now that the wedding had taken place he would carry on his affair with Mei-Ling. It was natural that he should love her because Mei-Ling was beautiful and of his father's race, and she had borne him a son. Every man wanted a son, and she had read somewhere that in China boys were considered very valuable. Not wives. Never wives, especially if they were foreign devils with pink faces and red hair!

9

Chang Lee didn't return for the evening meal but the mandarin came in, apologising for his lateness, as Lucy was finishing her soup.

'There is much dismay over the continued rioting,' he explained as he took his seat and motioned Chin Su to serve him. 'The Empress feels that we ought to advise the members of the foreign legations to send their families home. They could take the ship from Tientsin.'

'I thought a ship had been fired on in the harbour there.'

'An unfortunate incident,' he said. 'We must mobilise the Imperial troops, but they are under strength, and nobody knows exactly how many Boxers there are. But I should not trouble you with politics. Have you enjoyed a pleasant day?'

'It has been very hot,' she evaded.

'The wind scorches the rice-fields and dries up the rivers,' he said sombrely. 'Did Chang Lee return?'

'He went out again to Mei-Ling,' Lucy said, raising her eyes to his face and seeing the flash of consternation there.

'You know of Mei-Ling?' he asked carefully, after a moment.

'I ought to have been told,' Lucy said. 'It was not fair to keep it from me.'

'It was dishonourable,' he said, 'but I feared you would refuse the offer of marriage if I told you of Mei-Ling and her son. You know of the child too?'

'Yes.'

'Tong Su, my grandson,' he said, his

lips curving downwards. 'Born out of wedlock, to a girl who was intended for the royal harem. He is three years old now. We believed that the Empress, having forbidden Mei-Ling and my son to wed had allowed the matter to drop, but she was only biding her time. We could not tell you at once, but I hoped that you and Chang Lee—' He paused, a certain wistfulness in his gaze.

'I intend to be a good wife to your son,' Lucy said firmly.

Silently she added to herself. 'If I am given the opportunity.'

'You are a fine young woman,' Chang Lee said approvingly. 'My son is a fortunate man.'

Not so fortunate, Lucy reflected soberly. It must be dreadful to love one person and be forced to marry another. It was just as bad to fall in love with one's husband when he was already bound to another woman.

'You must give Chang Lee many sons,' the mandarin was saying. 'In that way a wife brings honour to the family and earns the respect of the husband.'

Lucy was tempted to say, 'First catch your husband and lock the bedroom door,' but the remark would have been in bad taste, so she remained silent, nibbling at the crisply fried noodles on her plate. No doubt Mei-Ling was serving Chang Lee some exotic delicacy and he was asking her how the child had come to fall and promising to visit them more often in future. Lucy's mouth tightened slightly. Her brief mood of despair was hardening into determination. She would make Chang Lee desire her and then Mei-Ling could take her sweet, mocking smile back to the royal harem where she had been intended to be. Aunt Harriet, if she could have seen her niece at that moment, would have declared that Lucy had her 'mule face' on!

The meal over she went up to her room again, thinking wryly that the apartment was becoming a refuge for her. At least she could be private here, and she drew the long curtains across the windows so that she wouldn't chance to see Chang Lee coming back across the courtyard. When she finally climbed into bed, however, she realised to her annoyance that she was listening for his footsteps. Impatiently she pulled the covers up round her ears and counted sheep until, out of sheer boredom, she fell asleep at last.

The morning brought a smiling Yang Fei with the breakfast tray, and Yang Chi with hot water. Lucy felt as she often did in the mornings before the promise of the day was broken. Sleep had refreshed her and replenished her energy. Even Mei-Ling had shrunk to a tiny cloud on the horizon.

'You wish to learn Mandarin this morning?' Yang Fei inquired.

'Yes, I do, but first I must speak to Prince Chang Lee.' She had resolved to make it clear to him that she knew about Mei-Ling and the reason he had married a foreigner, and that she would be ready to be full wife to him when he was ready to be a faithful husband. No doubt a Chinese wife would accept the situation meekly, but Lucy was neither weak nor Chinese. If this strange marriage was to have any chance of success then she must establish herself firmly as a personality in her own right.

'Prince Chang Lee left the house early this morning,' Yang Fei said. 'There is a meeting of the Council.'

'To talk about the riots?' Lucy said.

'I think so, princess. They are very bad men,' said Yang Fei solemnly. 'They make such trouble for everybody.'

If she thought it strange that husband

and wife still occupied separate bedrooms she was too polite to say so. It occurred to Lucy, as she sipped her tea, that she had never seen any of the other bedrooms in this large house. It would have been interesting to divine something of Chang Lee's tastes from the furnishings of his room, but it was probable that if she went exploring Chen Sula would walk in on her and try to make mischief out of the incident.

The day passed quietly. Yang Fei laboured earnestly to imprint a few simple phrases of Mandarin in Lucy's memory and, for all her politeness, could not refrain from giggling when her mistress attempted to pronounce them.

There was a small sewing-room at the end of the hall with some half finished pieces of embroidery in one of the cupboards. Lucy took out a red cushion cover with unfinished lotus flowers on it, selected some silks and, having eaten a solitary lunch, carried the work into the library.

The afternoon had half worn away when Chang Lee walked in, and for a moment she felt confused as if he were a stranger and she were seeing him for the first time.

'My father tells me you know about Mei-Ling?' he said, without greeting.

'It was my right to know,' she said calmly, hoping that he wasn't aware of the sudden beating of her heart.

'In China a woman has few rights,' he said.

'Men don't seem to have many rights here either,' she said sweetly, 'since they marry where they are bidden.'

'It is preferable to execution,' he said wryly. Lucy was inclined to agree with him, but obstinately kept silent, bending her head demurely over her sewing.

'If my father had failed to find a wife he would never have dared to return home,' Chang Lee was continuing.

'But he travelled ahead of me,' she said, 'I might have changed my mind.'

'Oh, he was certain that you would not,' Chang Lee said. 'My father assured me that, as it was unlikely anybody else would ever ask you, you would be glad to marry me.'

'Why wouldn't anybody else ask me?' she demanded.

'He said you had no dowry and red

hair.' Chang Lee gave her a kindly look, adding. 'For my own part, I am becoming accustomed to it!'

'Oh, good! I was worrying,' she said bitingly.

'And you are learning Mandarin and sewing.' He glanced at her work.

'I can be very domesticated,' Lucy told him. 'And I must find something to occupy my time.'

'Chen Sula will be pleased that someone is finishing those covers,' he remarked. 'Her duties give her little free time.'

So the embroidery belonged to the housekeeper. Lucy felt a sudden distaste for the gaudy red silk.

'Did you have a good Council meeting?' she asked, seeking to change the subject.

'I am not a full member of the Council,' he said, 'but T'zu Hsi commanded all to attend. She expressed shock at the attacks being made by the Boxers on foreigners and on Christian Chinese. She has also promised that when the leaders of the movement are found they will be severely punished.'

'And do you believe her?' Lucy asked.

'The Empress is inclined to say one thing in public and another in private. I believe she sympathises, as many of us do, with nationalist aims.'

Lucy remembered the implacable faces and glinting eyes of the men who had stopped the wagon on her way from Tientsin and shivered.

'There is nothing to fear,' he said. 'The Forbidden City is well guarded.'

'I'm not afraid,' she said promptly, her green eyes meeting his defiantly.

'What troubles me is I am called to the Winter Palace so often that I have no time to spend with you,' he said abruptly. 'I would like to know you better!'

'So that you can compare me with Mei-Ling,' she inquired lightly. 'She is exceedingly pretty.'

'Exceedingly,' he agreed, a speculative gleam in his black eyes as they rested on her.

'One must only hope that she doesn't run to fat as she grows older,' Lucy murmured.

'A little flesh is attractive in a woman,' Chang Lee said.

'And Tong Su? Is he better today?'

'It was only a graze. He's at the age when he likes climbing and running and doesn't see any danger.'

Lucy heard that softened note in his voice and her heart sank again. Given time she believed she could capture Chang Lee's affections from his Chinese mistress, but she couldn't compete with a small child. There would always be that link between himself and Mei-Ling.

'You would have been informed of their existence when you had settled in your new home,' he said.

'When I had become meek and submissive, like a good little Chinese wife?'

She stabbed her needle viciously through the red silk.

'You misunderstand me,' he said, a pucker between his brows.

'As you misunderstand me.' She set her work aside and rose, facing him with her head held high. 'I did not expect love in this marriage but I did expect honesty. You should have been honest and explained the situation when I arrived here!'

'And would you have stayed?' he demanded.

'I don't know.' She spread her hands, shaking her head. 'So much has happened so quickly that I can't think clearly any more. All I know is that it's an impossible situation.'

'Surely not unknown, even in England,' he countered.

'I'm aware of that but in England husbands don't make a habit of keeping their mistresses at the bottom of the garden!' she retorted.

'Mei-Ling is no longer my mistress. She has not been for more than a year.'

'Then why did the Empress order you to marry a foreigner?'

'The Empress,' he said, 'has a long memory and a peculiar twist of humour. My father took a foreign devil as a wife, and so it was fitting that his son should marry one too, especially since he had had the temerity to fall in love with a girl intended to become a royal concubine.'

'And you don't care for Mei-Ling any longer?' she ventured.

'Of course I care!' he said impatiently. 'She was my first love and no young man forgets his first love affair. There is a reckless sweetness in it, the more so in our case because Mei-Ling and I were not permitted to marry. If we had become husband and wife then we could have settled down, watched our love deepen and grow. But young men grow up and the sweetness loses a little of its savour.

'But she still lives so near!'

'Her father was our steward and built the house. She has a right to live in her father's house.'

'And you visit her.'

'Would you have me toss aside the mother of my child?' he asked. 'She needs a protector, someone to advise her and keep her company from time to time.'

'And you like to see the boy,' Lucy said.

'Even in China a man is expected to honour his obligations,' Chang Lee said.

'And you still have a fondness for her. It's very natural.' Lucy tried to speak reasonably and sensibly but, to her horror, her voice quavered. She hastily turned to pick up the sewing, hearing his voice through a blurred confusion of feelings.

'I am shamed by the trick that was played upon you. My father and I thought only of ourselves when you were brought here. You have shown yourself truly understanding and I thank you for it.'

He went out before she could frame an answer and she sat down again abruptly, shielding her face with her hand. She was beginning to understand more than he realised himself. He was attracted to her and in time she might hope to win him, but Mei-Ling and the child stood in the way, and Mei-Ling resented the advent of this foreign wife as Chen Sula had resented Chang Marie. Lucy couldn't find it in her heart to blame either of them, but it made her own position almost intolerable. She was falling in love with Chang Lee and that alone made her vulnerable.

'Are you sick, princess?' Yang Fei asked from the open doorway.

Her kind little face was full of friendly concern.

'It is the heat, I think,' Lucy said, straightening up. 'There's no moisture.'

'People from other lands often grow sick in the heat,' Yang Fei said. 'In the winter it is very cold, and some of them grow sick then too.'

'There's no pleasing the foreign devils, is there?' Lucy said, forcing a smile.

'Oh, you do not seem like a foreigner to me!' Yang Fei exclaimed. 'You are a very kind lady, very polite, not like a barbarian at all!'

'Am I indeed!' Lucy laughed in earnest,

though there was a wryness in her mirth.

She was constantly being reminded that here, in Peking, it was she who was the foreigner, the stranger.

'You are feeling better now?' the girl questioned, looking puzzled.

'Yang Fei, you are a joy and a delight to me!' Lucy exclaimed. 'I swear I'll make you my housekeeper one day!'

'Chen Sula is housekeeper,' Yang Fei said gravely. 'The mandarin would not allow such a thing!'

'Where is Chen Sula? I have not seen her all day.'

'She has gone to the Mongol market beyond the walls to order food and wine,' Yang Fei said. 'Many people are buying more food lest there be famine later. The Boxers, too, steal food when it is being carried into the city. The times are very bad, princess.'

There is no apparent sign of trouble, Lucy thought, when she came down for the evening meal. The long table was set with its crystal and china; course after course of elaborately spiced food was served, and beyond the windows only the tinkling of the wind bells could be heard. The House of the Willow was an enchanted place where no danger or hardship seemed to threaten.

As if by mutual consent the conversation was kept on a light and trivial level, the mandarin relating some frivolous anecdotes of his youth, Chang Lee propounding some Chinese riddles. Lucy felt her nebulous fears dissipating. No doubt there was often civil strife in such an enormous country and Yang Fei had probably exaggerated when she had spoken of possible food shortages.

'The Feast of the Moon Mother will be upon us before we know it,' Chang Lee remarked.

'The Moon Mother?' Lucy looked at him inquiringly.

'Kwan Yin in her aspect as goddess of the moon,' he explained. 'The feast is held twice a year at the time of a full moon, and the Empress has signified her intention of holding the festival as usual.'

'If the rain comes,' Chang Lee said, 'we may regard the festival as a success. Certainly it will be interesting for you to see it, Lucy. We will go together if that pleases you.'

So he sought her company in public at least. She smiled at him, wishing there could always be this harmony between them.

'You have not been to the market yet,' his father said. 'Chin Shu is ready to escort you at any time.'

'Yes, I know, but from what you said I began to wonder whether it was wise or not,' she said.

'Oh, you'll be safe enough,' Chang Lee said. 'The market people dislike the Boxers as much as anybody else, because they depend on the foreigners for much of their trade. You must buy what you want, my dear Lucy.'

He spoke with the kindliness of a friend but not with the ardour of a lover, she thought. That might come later if she could make him forget Mei-Ling and the bonds that united him to his boyhood sweetheart.

The meal over they went into the long drawing-room and prepared for a quiet evening. The mandarin took out a delicately carved set of chess-men and invited his son to a game while Lucy sat at a low table and amused herself by looking through a book of watercolour paintings.

Frequently her attention wandered from the pastel brush-strokes delineating birds and flowers, and she glanced up towards the two men, watching their profiles shadowed against the wall. There was a marked resemblance between father and son, but Chang Liu's face betrayed a settled disillusionment with life. Lucy wished that there was something she could do to prevent that same expression from becoming habitual on Chang Lee's face. Already it was beginning to show weariness that caught at her heart.

'Checkmate!' Chang Liu said finally, satisfaction in his voice.

'You must allow me to beat you once or twice one day,' Chang Lee said, laughing as he leaned back in his chair.

'There's no merit in winning unless it's deserved,' Chang Liu retorted, 'and I have the advantage of many years' playing, my boy! Lucy, you must learn to play chess.'

'Yes, I must,' she said, and wondered if his words concealed a deeper advice, or if the atmosphere of this house was imprinting itself upon her, making her sense undercurrents of meaning—even in the simplest words.

'Lucy is already learning Chinese,' Chang Lee said, smiling at her. 'She must allow herself some time for pleasure.'

'I look forward to the Moon Festival,' she said eagerly.

'Let us hope that Kwan Yin will send us rain and increase the crops,' Chang Liu said, a shadow crossing his face. 'The heat and the dust are excessive for this time of year.'

'And the Boxers declare that they are signs of heaven's displeasure because all the foreigners have not been expelled from China,' his son said.

'I thought you shared that opinion,' Lucy said boldly.

'Motive but not method,' he said briefly. 'And not all foreigners. We have some charming ones among us.'

His smile and bow were in her direction and she accepted the compliment with a graceful little bow of her own. There was no doubt that his attitude towards her was softening. That was a beginning but there was still a long road to travel before he regarded her with the affection he cherished still for Mei-Ling. Involuntarily her head jerked up and she resolved privately that she would not allow herself to be held back by self-pity.

Chen Sula came in with a tray of tea and some fragrant biscuits, putting them down silently. It was the first time she had provided refreshments during the evening and Lucy suspected that curiosity had led her to bring them in. The housekeeper's eyes flickered from the two men at the chessboard to where Lucy sat, the book of watercolour drawings open at her hand. Something in the peacefulness of the scene evidently irritated her, for she made an impatient movement and said something in Chinese.

'Speak English,' Chang Lee interrupted. 'Lucy is with us.'

'Oh, pray don't trouble!' Lucy spoke amiably. 'I must get used to hearing Chinese spoken, so that I can begin to understand it. Otherwise I will never be able to direct the affairs of the household.'

The mandarin, she noticed, was looking at her with respect mingled with faint amusement. Chen Sula's face flushed darkly red but she pressed her lips together tightly.

'You seem to be making a conquest of Yang Fei already,' Chang Lee drawled. 'She is of the opinion that you are a most elegant and clever mistress!'

'And I have a high opinion of her,' Lucy said promptly. 'I am very grateful to you for letting me have her.'

'You are the mistress here, my dear Lucy. You must make what arrangements you please,' he returned.

'Am I to pour the tea?' Chen Sula interrupted in English.

'No need to trouble,' Lucy rose and went over to the tray. 'I can see to the mandarin's and my husband's needs. Thank you, Chen Sula.'

It was a dismissal and, for a moment, she wondered if the housekeeper would lose her temper. There was real hatred in the snapping black eyes and her fingers were clenched, the knuckles yellowish-white. Then she bowed and went out silently, and something dark lifted from the room.

Chang Lee came over to where Lucy stood, his hand outstretched to take the cup. Her own hand shook slightly as she poured the clear amber liquid. A battle had just been fought and won but one battle was not the whole war. In Chen Sula she had made a formidable enemy and her spirit quailed a little at the thought of the struggle that lay ahead.

10

The days were shaping themselves into a pattern. Lucy spent the mornings with Yang Fei, who had lost her first shyness and often dissolved into fits of giggles at her mistress's attempts to pronounce the Chinese tongue. At the midday meal she was frequently joined by the mandarin or by Chang Lee, both of whom were evidently expected to attend the Empress for part of each day. The long afternoons were devoted to reading and sewing, both occupations which grew wearisome after a time. More and more Lucy found herself, book or needlework on her lap, staring through the long window across the courtyard to where the trees tossed blossom-clad branches in the scorching wind. She suspected that Chang Lee went every day to the house at the other side of the orchard and a little dart of jealousy pierced her. She had never been in love before, but she recognised the symptoms of it in herself, and felt curiously vulnerable. The man whom she had come to marry was proving more attractive than she had dreamed, and, in a strange way, this made it harder for her to establish herself as his wife.

The evenings had become family affairs, with the three of them retiring after dinner to the pleasant drawing-room where the two men played chess or Chang Lee initiated her into the mysteries of mah-jong. Those were hours that she valued greatly, for it seemed to her that every word and every smile fashioned another link that bound them more closely. Given time, she sensed that she could bind him as closely as Mei-Ling had done, but there were moments when she wondered if there would be time. Chang Liu, full of an elderly man's pessimism, talked of the Boxer uprisings that were becoming more serious as day followed day. The danger to foreigners and to the Christian Chinese was becoming more intense, and the supply lines were often cut by the rioters so that food was arriving in a trickle instead of its usual flood.

'Members of the foreign legations have been advised to leave while they still can,' he said sombrely, 'but they insist on remaining.'

'Even if they left now we have no guarantee they would reach Tientsin safely,' Chang Lee said. 'The entire army is already under strength and I'd not lay wagers on the loyalty of all the officers either! No, don't look alarmed, Lucy. If the danger becomes excessive I will make plans to have you taken to the hills where you will be safe.'

'No!' She looked up sharply. 'I'll not be bundled away like a child. My home is here now.'

He made no answer but his glance at her was an admiring one. Lucy felt her cheeks flush with pleasure. In only a few days the young man burning with resentment at being forced to wed a foreigner had become accustomed to her presence. Now it would not be her fault if she couldn't make him forget Mei-Ling and fall in love with her.

The festival of Full Moon was almost upon them. Mindful of her resolve to wear Chinese dress Lucy decided to visit the market. Since her arrival in the Forbidden City she had not been beyond the walls and, despite the heat and the dust, she stepped out eagerly with Chen Shu at her side. The manservant had apparently accepted her presence without difficulty, and Lucy wondered if his journey to England had caused him to regard foreigners with more tolerance than his countrymen did. His bland face and quietly respectful voice gave no indication of his private thoughts.

Despite the heat it was pleasant to be taking a walk again and she stepped along briskly, shielded by her parasol. The Forbidden City lay like a jewel within its massive walls, their stark grandeur softened by the fruit-trees and spiky bamboos. As they approached the Ha Ta gate the hum that beat increasingly upon her eardrums intensified into the shrieking of market-sellers, the rattling of wheels over cobbles, the clashing of arms as a squad of soldiers drilled.

A small door at the side of the main entrance was open and they passed through and were immediately swallowed up in a mass of jostling people. Smells and sounds assailed her from all sides at once, and Lucy hesitated for a moment, bewildered by the abrupt transition from peace to noise.

There were stalls everywhere, their counters protected from the sun by striped awnings and piled high with goods. Heaps of shiny-skinned fruit and vegetables met her gaze. If there was a food shortage it was not yet apparent here. Those who had no stalls had spread out their wares on cloths laid across the cobbles, and others had large baskets hung round their necks and walked up and down, raising their voices in what was evidently a description of the goods they were trying to sell.

Apart from the foodstuffs there were bolts of cotton and silk, piles of bowls and cups in brilliantly patterned china, carved animals and figurines, boxes of tea, dyed feathers and grasses, ivories, trinkets of jade, squat jars of coloured ink with long brushes tied to the handles. The valuable and the gimcrack, durable and perishable, were mingled in apparent confusion, and the noise was deafening.

In Peking it was evidently the custom to buy and sell at the top of one's voice. Up and down the narrow aisles left between the stalls the people jostled, laughed, bargained and gaped. Men sat cross-legged in the middle of it all, rolling dice and adding their own voices to the din. At one side, in a roped space, cages of songbirds twittered unceasingly.

Lucy's eyes moved in fascinated attention from one vignette to the next. This was the Orient she had imagined, this vulgar, colourful, noisy, bustling stew of humanity, arguing and laughing, buying, selling, gambling, as she stood rapt in contemplation of it all.

'Princess, you wish to buy very fine silk?' Chin Shu was inquiring. 'Tan Ho has the best in the market. It is expensive but very fine.'

'Yes. Yes, I do.' She had to raise her voice to make herself heard.

Chin Shu touched her on the arm, nodding towards a booth that was set back from the others.

It was evidently a permanent structure, a door at the side leading into a wooden building not much larger than a hut but containing a long table and two stools. As they stepped into the cool interior a small, plump man came forward, bowing. From the tone of his voice it was evident that he knew Chin Shu, and Lucy waited while greetings were exchanged between the two men.

'Tan Ho bids you welcome to his humble

place of business,' Chin Shu translated for her. 'He begs you to do the honour of taking tea with him while he shows you some of his unworthy goods.'

'Tell him that I am happy to accept.' Lucy returned the other's bow and seated herself on one of the stools. This was obviously going to be a politely prolonged affair.

The tea, served with lemon, had a delicately refreshing tang. Sipping it, Lucy watched with interest as bolts of silk were unrolled on the table. Silk so fine that it looked transparent. Heavy silk embroidered with gold and silver thread. Silk that was dyed in vivid shades of scarlet, lemon, emerald and aquamarine. Silk that shaped itself into graceful folds as Tan Ho's fat little hands unrolled it. Her eyes were dazzled by the colour and beauty.

'Tan Ho regrets he has nothing finer. If he had known you were coming he would have tried to find something more worthy of the bride of Prince Chang Lee,' Chin Shu translated.

There was a roll of black silk shot through with faint threads of silver like moonlight on dark water, and a heavier silk of grey-green with a tiny pearl woven at intervals into the material. Lucy set down her cup and pointed to them, nodding and smiling to indicate approval. More tea was brought and she drank it while Chin Shu and Tan Ho settled down to the pleasurable business of bargaining, a process accompanied by sighs, groans, eyes raised to heaven, and eventually a positive flurry of bows.

She wondered a little guiltily if the purchases had been as expensive as she feared and then reminded herself that it was being charged to the mandarin's account and that Chang Liu could probably afford to buy Tan Ho's entire stock.

The silk carefully wrapped and entrusted to Chin Shu, more tea politely offered and as politely declined, and the transaction was over. They were bowed out of the door into the pandemonium of the market again.

'Will you buy sandals?' Chin Shu asked.

Lucy nodded and he turned at once into another alley, going a little ahead of her to elbow the crowd out of the way.

Following in his wake, Lucy noticed that these market people were too intent on their own business to pay much attention to her, and when anyone did meet her eye they dropped their own gaze and moved aside. Foreign devils were tolerated but not much liked, she concluded ruefully.

Shoes and sandals of wood, leather, felt and raffia were heaped on the ground next to the sandalmaker's stall. There was a bench where she sat while she tried on various items of footwear and Chin Shu embarked on another long bargaining session with the elderly man who bustled forward to serve them. A pair of low-heeled black sandals and a similar pair in dull red leather were fitted, approved and wrapped, and she walked on at a leisurely pace, vowing that she would pay closer heed to Yang Fei's teaching and so reach the stage when she could speak sufficient Chinese to conduct her own shopping. Languages raised barriers as thick as stone between human beings.

'You wish your fortune told?' Chin Shu was pointing towards a wooden booth. Within its dim confines an old man sat cross-legged behind a low table.

'I'd not be able to understand it,' she said regretfully.

'This one speaks English. I will explain and pay him.'

The manservant hurried forward, and a few moments later she found herself bending under the low doorway into the booth.

'Please to sit, Princess Chang Lucy.' The old man's voice was high and thin, like wind sighing through reeds.

She squatted awkwardly, noting out of the corner of her eye that Chin Shu had wandered off, tactfully, to look at some ivories displayed on a nearby stall.

'Please to throw the yarrow sticks six times,' the man said.

Lucy took the bundle of polished sticks and scattered them over the surface of the table. The man was writing something on a piece of paper, tongue between teeth as he inked the symbols.

'Again, if you please.' He spoke without looking up. Meekly she collected the sticks together and tossed them again. They rolled over the table, making little clicking noises as they came to rest, and the old man formed his symbols and said, 'Again,' in his high reedy voice. There was something queerly hypnotic in the atmosphere of the place and the noises of the bright market were curiously muted.

The fortune-teller looked up and began

to speak, his tone almost a chant, his long eyes hooded beneath their yellowish lids.

'The meaning of the prophecy is Ta Kuo, trees hidden beneath a marsh. Princess, you stand alone in a place where you are a stranger. Take care, for you are still in a position of weakness. Alone you can do little. Enemies. Many tears.'

'It doesn't sound very cheerful.' She tried to speak lightly but her voice shook.

'On the night of the willow,' the old man said, ignoring the interruption, 'on that night a flower will grow from the withered trunk and your weakness will become strength. More I cannot tell.'

She had no wish to hear more. The words made no sense but they roused echoes in her mind like harps heard under water.

'More I cannot tell,' he repeated.

She muttered a bewildered 'thank you' and rose, suddenly wanting to know more but not knowing what questions to ask. The old man was gathering the sticks into a bundle again, muttering softly to himself, not looking at her.

She stepped out into the sunshine again, blinking in the glare, and looked round for Chin Shu. He had moved farther along the row of stalls, and it was a moment before she spotted him, his head bent over some trinkets, the packages still under his arm.

Snapping open her parasol, she was about to move towards him when there was a sudden stir in the milling crowd and the sound of hoofbeats across the cobbles. She had stepped back to avoid the rush as a group of people streamed down the alley, shouting and gesticulating as they ran. There was a blur of faces and waving arms, a crash as one of the booths was overturned, scattering oranges all over the ground, a glint of sunlight along the blade of a curved sword.

Lucy pressed against the side of a booth, raised her eyes and looked straight into the broad face of the shaven headed Boxer who sat his pony insolently grinning as he slashed with his sword at the ropes that held the striped awnings taut. It was the man who had stopped the wagon on its way from Tientsin. Until that moment she had not realised how clearly she remembered the sneering face, the red band tied round the shaven skull with its long pigtail.

Terror iced her spine and then she was running with the rest, the parasol jerked from her hand, her dress dragging on the cobbles. Behind her was the splintering of wood, the repeated cries of *'Hai! Hai!'* the shrill screaming of the fleeing crowd.

She blundered into another alley, tripping over a pile of broken china as she ran, her breath sobbing in her throat. In her panic she had lost all sense of direction, but this was not a part of the market through which she had previously walked. There were sacks of grain and rice spilling out on to the cobbles, and tall jars of blossom set between the stalls. Others were running the same way. For one horrifying moment she was caught up in a swirl of blue tunics and pigtails and pointing fingers. She tore herself free from the grasp of clutching fingers, kicked aside a pile of melons and ran again, twisting and turning away between two wooden huts, and hammered with her fists on the door that loomed up before her.

There was an agonising pause as the cries behind her swelled closer. Then a bolt scraped back and she was pulled within and the door slammed shut again. The man who had admitted her was Chinese but clad in the dark suit of a European. He stepped back a pace, looking her up and down with an expression of such disbelief on his face that she was startled into hysterical laughter.

She was in a small courtyard with an archway leading to a larger one. There were high walls all about her with narrow shuttered windows. That much she glimpsed before footsteps sounded and Stephen Just hurried towards them.

'Lucy!' He used her Christian name, his pleasant face shocked. 'What happened to you?'

Her hat was crooked, the hem of her skirt torn, a long lock of hair tumbled from its pins, her face dripping with perspiration. She was suddenly absurdly conscious of the fright she must look.

'What happened?' Stephen repeated.

'Boxers,' she said gaspingly. 'In the market-place, knocking over the stalls. Everyone was running and I ran with them.'

'My dear lady!' He took her hands in his own firm grasp. 'What a terrible experience for you! But what were you doing in the Mongol quarter in the first place? Few Europeans venture there without escort these days.'

'Chin Shu, the manservant, was with

me. We were separated when the Boxers arrived.'

'You must come and sit down,' he urged, taking her arm and saying something to the other man in Chinese as he guided her away.

'Where are we?' She looked round in a vain attempt to get her bearings.

'In the main Legation compound. The British ambassador, Sir Claud MacDonald, has ordered all British nationals to move within the walls. We are extremely crowded already and more are arriving everyday. I'm sharing a room with one of the Belgian attachés and we've been warned to make space for a third gentleman. This way.'

They were entering a narrow street, bedecked with various national flags. Under their feet the yellow dust rose in clouds, and Stephen Just grimaced as he ushered her up a couple of steps into a high-ceilinged apartment.

'I'll have hot water and some towels brought up at once,' he said. 'One of the maids will tend to your needs. I must go and find out what is happening.'

She was being shown into a small bedroom with a neat, almost military precision in the arrangement of the furnishings. Stephen, with a last, reassuring squeeze of her arm, hurried out. Lucy sat down on the edge of the narrow bed and shivered, aware that she was shaking violently. Now that her panic was subsiding her legs felt as weak as water. There was a tap on the door and a small Chinese girl came in, staggering under the weight of a large jug and a pile of fleecy towels. In her wake hovered a plump woman of indeterminate age whose rigidly corseted bosom betrayed a certain agitation.

'Princess Chang Lucy, is it not? I am Cecily Bainbridge, my dear. Young Mr Just has told me of your misadventure. Most unwise of you to venture beyond the walls, but I suppose, as the wife of a—Chinese, you felt satisfied in taking the risk. We had heard of your arrival, of course, and wondered when you would call to pay your respects to the ambassador.'

Her voice was high and slightly nasal, her eyes inquisitive as they roved over Lucy's dishevelled frame. The girl felt uncomfortable under the raking stare and turned gratefully to the bowl where the Chinese maid had poured the steaming water.

'You may go, Tina,' Mrs Bainbridge said, clapping her hands sharply.

The maidservant bowed and pattered out.

'One must be firm with these people otherwise they take advantage,' Mrs Bainbridge said. 'Three years I've spent in Peking and I can't honestly say I would trust one of them if it came to a conflict of loyalties. Oh, the higher classes are quite like us, I believe, but you will know that, being married to one of them.'

'To Prince Chang Lee.' Lucy groped for the towel and rubbed her face.

'I believe that Mr Just is acquainted with the prince. His father is said to be immensely rich?'

There was a faint question in her voice but Lucy ignored it, dragging the pins out of her hair and reaching for the comb in her pocket.

'There are American Marines on their way here to teach those Boxers a lesson,' the other said. 'One of those little native risings it is, of course, but they can be most upsetting! Your husband's house is within the Forbidden City, I believe. Only Chinese are permitted there, of course, unless they have special invitation, and very few of the Chinese have laid eyes on the Empress.'

'I was received in audience the day after I arrived,' Lucy said, stung into boastfulness.

'By the Empress? What is she like? They say she's a terrible old woman.'

'She is very powerful, very regal,' Lucy said slowly.

'That was where you met Mr Just, of course! He mentioned an execution.'

'A beheading,' Lucy said shortly. 'I saw it.'

'My dear, how perfectly dreadful! They will take centuries to civilise of course! Ah, here is Mr Just! I have elected myself as chaperon, Mr Just, lest there be any scandal about a bachelor gentleman entertaining a married lady.'

Her tone was arch, but Stephen answered her expressionlessly, his eyes moving to Lucy with open admiration.

'Very kind of you, Mrs Bainbridge. Are you feeling better, Lucy? I don't think the riot was a serious one, but it was certainly too close for comfort. Will you have some lunch before you return? I will have an escort for you, of course, after such an experience you ought to rest for a while.'

'I really don't think I can spare the time for luncheon,' Cecily Bainbridge fluted.

'Princess Chang Lucy and I will contrive to manage alone,' Stephen said coolly. 'Thank you for coming over. Please convey my respects to your husband. I will see him at the ambassador's this evening, I hope?'

'At the celebration party? Yes of course. We wouldn't miss it for worlds.'

She was bowing to Lucy and being gradually edged to the door by the politely determined young man. Lucy, seating herself in a small antechamber off the main hall, wanted to laugh.

'Mrs Bainbridge's name ought to be Busybody,' Stephen remarked, coming back and sitting next to her. 'She is an excellent woman but she will insist on having a finger in every pie.'

'What celebration is it?' Lucy asked.

The little maid had returned and was setting chicken salad before them.

'Mafeking has been relieved,' he said, looking faintly surprised. 'Three months ago, but the news only reached us a couple of days ago. It looks as if we finally have the Boers on the run!'

'Isn't it their country too?' she asked slowly.

'They consider it to be, but one cannot build an empire by seeing the other fellow's point of view,' Stephen said. 'It is our duty to protect and civilise other nations.'

Lucy, contrasting Cecily Bainbridge's overdressed, overbearing presence with the classical simplicity and politeness of the Chinese, felt a sudden sympathy for the Boxers.

'I had hoped to see you again before this,' Stephen said, leaning to pour wine for her.

'Oh, I am kept fully occupied,' she said brightly. 'I am learning Mandarin, though it is uphill work.'

'I learned sufficient at college to make myself understood,' Stephen said, 'but I cannot read or write it. Few of the ordinary Chinese can. And what else do you do?'

'Oh, this and that,' she said, and took a mouthful of chicken.

'And are you settling down? You are happy?' His eyes and voice were full of kindly concern, penetrating her guard.

Abruptly she said. 'Did you know about Mei-Ling? Did you know why the Empress ordered the mandarin to find a European bride for his son?'

'Peking is always full of rumour,' he

began uneasily. 'I wondered if such a marriage had any chance of success. Of course, it might be possible to have it annulled, if the parties concerned were not content!'

'It will be a good marriage,' she said firmly. 'Chang Lee is—very kind to me.'

'Just remember that you have friends to whom you can turn, and are not alone in a foreign land,' he said.

'Thank you.' She smiled, thinking how strange it was that, within a very short time, she had begun to feel more at home among the Chinese than with her own countrymen.

The maid, Tina, had bowed herself out. They were alone in the pleasant little sitting-room with only the noises from the street to disturb their peacefulness.

Now Tina pattered back, a taller figure standing behind her. Lucy, catching sight of Chang Lee, put down her fork and rose thankfully.

'Chang Lee! Is the riot over? How did you know I was here?'

'One of the servants was in the market and saw you running to the Legation.' He put his hands on her shoulders and gave her a keen, searching look. 'Were you hurt or merely alarmed?'

'She was badly shaken,' Stephen said.

'Well, it doesn't appear to have spoiled her appetite,' Chang Lee said dryly, glancing at the table. 'The riot was no more than a show of defiance and the only casualties a few broken heads. What will you do when the Boxers arrive in force?'

'Do you really think they will?' Stephen said.

'I'm certain of it, and so would you be, if you weren't living in a fool's paradise,' Chang Lee said briefly. 'Put your hat on, Lucy. Chin Shu is so busy blaming himself for losing you that he is quite useless at his duties.'

'May we expect you at the reception this evening?' Stephen asked.

'I think Lucy has had enough excitement for one day.' Chang Lee bowed, a faint chill in his manner. 'Thank you for your care of her.'

'You will remember that you are welcome at any time?' Stephen said to her.

'You're very kind.' She returned his bow, conscious of his eyes on her. This young man admired her and, given encouragement, might grow into a warmer feeling. A year before she might have been flattered and tempted, but now she was Chang Lee's bride and there was no room in her heart for any other man.

In the narrow street she glanced up at Chang Lee's set face and said crossly, 'You might have been better pleased to see me! I could have been quite badly hurt!'

'Not at the speed you were making for the Legation. You seem to have outstripped every Boxer in sight in your eagerness to have luncheon with Stephen Just.'

'I lost my sense of direction and didn't even know it was the Legation,' she argued. 'And I thought Mr Just was a friend of yours.'

'He certainly seems to be a friend of my wife,' he returned sourly.

For a moment she was tempted to reply sharply, but an imp of mischief was dancing in her green eyes. So Chang Lee already cared sufficiently for her to be jealous when another man paid her attention.

'I find him charming,' she said sweetly, slipping her arm through his as they crossed to the gate. 'You are so often on court business or visiting—friends, it ought to be a comfort to you to know that I won't lack an escort if I wish to go out somewhere.'

'We will none of us be going out unless the Boxers are curbed,' he said grimly, 'and when we do, you will be escorted by your husband like a good Chinese wife!'

'And when you visit Mei-Ling,' she said softly, 'will you require my company then?'

She had not expected a reply and he made none, but she had the satisfaction of noting that he had flushed darkly.

11

To Lucy's relief Chin Shu had kept tight hold of the purchases, and the lengths of silk were safely wrapped up in her room when she returned. Yang Fei hurried to meet her, stammering her relief at her safe return in a mixture of Chinese and English that was as comical as it was touching. Chin Shu was also there, bowing and apologising, and when Lucy had changed her dress she came down to be greeted by the mandarin.

'I hastened back from the Winter Palace to see for myself that you were unharmed, my dear,' he said warmly.

'I was more frightened than anything,' she reassured him.

'The situation is exceedingly grave,' he frowned. 'I voted with those of the Council who want general mobilisation against the Boxers, but the Empress will say neither yea nor nay.'

'Our people are not trained for fighting,' Chang Lee said. 'Most of them are peasant farmers, working their land as best they can in the face of famine, rapacious landlords, foreign interference—I beg your pardon, Lucy, but it's true.'

'The Boxers will ruin China much more quickly than any foreigners,' his father said.

'And Lucy must stay within the walls until the troubles are over,' Chang Lee said. 'I'd not have a moment's peace if I thought she was wandering about all over the place!'

His expression was as grim as the tone of his voice, but her pulse leapt as she heard his words. Perhaps after all she was becoming valuable to him even if he was not fully prepared to admit it.

When she went up to her room that night Chen Sula was waiting for her. The housekeeper's sloe black eyes were cold as she bowed.

'You were not safe, princess, to venture outside. I warned you that our people did not like foreign devils.'

'These were Boxers,' Lucy said with equal coldness. 'The market people took no notice of me.'

'They are accustomed to foreigners,' Chen Sula said, a faint contempt in her tone.

'Was there anything particular you wished to say to me?' Lucy asked.

'Chin Shu informed me you had bought some materials in the market-place. Are you going to have them made up into gowns?'

'Straight robes in the mandarin style,' Lucy said.

'Like a fashionable Chinese lady.'

There was no mistaking the sneer in her voice, and Lucy felt her temper begin to rise.

'I believe one should adopt the customs of the country,' she said stiffly.

'So that Chang Lee will fall in love with you?'

Chen Sula had dropped her voice to a whisper as she moved closer. 'Do you really believe that is possible? It is Mei-Ling who has held his heart since he was a boy. Oh, he is very kind to you. He is very kind to the English devil whom the Empress forced him to marry, but it is Mei-Ling whom he goes to see. It is my daughter who waits for him in her house beyond the orchard. It is Mei-Ling who bore him a son. How will you ever bear him sons when he never comes to your bed?'

'Get out!' Lucy heard her own voice thickening with rage. 'Get out and leave me alone. You're not wanted here.'

'It is you who is not wanted,' Chen Sula said, insultingly gentle. 'It is you who ought to go away, back to your own country.'

She withdrew before the other could frame a reply, but her words had cast a shadow over Lucy's newborn hopes. For a moment she shivered, aware of the task that lay ahead. Then she moved resolutely to the parcels and untied them, letting the silk ripple over her fingers. She would ask Yang Fei to help her with the cutting out of the pattern and the stitching, and she would wear one of the new robes at the Moon Festival.

Yang Fei, when appealed to, said obligingly that she and her sister would be happy to make the gowns.

'For the Moon Feast is in one week, so we must hasten and yet not spoil the work,' she said, her thin little hands touching the silk gently. 'You will look most beautiful, princess.'

Lucy hoped that Chang Lee would think so and was immediately anxious to begin the work. The sewing-room being Chen Sula's province she took over the study, and the long afternoons were spent peacefully cutting out and stitching in the big, cool apartment. Chang Lee looked in on them from time to time and went away again, smiling a little as if the sight of his industrious wife pleased him. Lucy, taking tiny tucks round the high neckline of a robe, hoped that he was not imagining her content to let matters drift on between them with nothing resolved. Her own feelings towards him grew warmer as day followed day and she could have sworn that the friendship between them was growing stronger, but friendship was not love. Often, when it was too warm to sleep, she lay wakeful in the big bed, wondering if Chang Lee occupied his own or stole through the orchard to visit Mei-Ling, and when the day came she was always too proud to ask him.

The American Marines had marched in to prepare defences for the Legation.

'Only seventy-five men,' Chang Lee said wryly, 'and they'll be hard pressed to find sufficient ammunition and rations for that number. The market people fear to sell to the Europeans lest they incur Boxer reprisals.'

'And what is the Empress doing?' Lucy demanded.

'Urging calm and preparing for the Moon Festival,' he said, without hesitation.

It was unladylike to snort but she came near to doing so. T'zu Hsi obviously ran with the hare and hunted with the hounds, giving no clear lead to her people. The Royal Guard was being called out daily for extra duty. Lucy heard snatches of marching feet and shouted commands above the cooing of the doves, and one evening, as they sat at table, she was startled by a far off booming that might have been thunder but was too regular for that.

'Cannon in the harbour,' Chang Lee said briefly. 'The noise travels faster at night.'

'Then the way out of Peking is blocked,' she said, trying to sound as if the question was of merely academic interest.

'It is still possible for you to be escorted up into the hills until the trouble is over,' the mandarin said.

'My place is here, with my husband,' she said, raising her voice slightly, for she had glimpsed Chen Sula in the hall beyond.

Since her extraordinary outburst the house-keeper had avoided her, confining herself to her own quarters and the kitchen. Once or twice Lucy had caught sight of her crossing the courtyard, presumably from a visit to her daughter, but by tacit consent the comings and goings of the older woman remained unremarked.

Thanks to the tireless industry of Yang Fei and Yang Chi the two robes were ready in good time, Lucy held them up against herself in delight. For the Moon Festival she would wear the black one. High-necked with sleeves that widened from throat to hem, glinting faint silver as she moved.

The feast was to begin at dusk, but the feeling of special occasion was with Lucy when she woke and stayed with her throughout the day. In the kitchen they were baking crescent-shaped cakes of rice and honey, and in the hall two of the servants were hanging up garlands of white and silver.

When the time came to dress Yang Fei came up to help her. Lucy had enjoyed a leisurely bath and was now in the black robe. She had left off the tight corset that nipped in her waist under the close fitting bodices of her Western dresses, and felt an unaccustomed sense of freedom in the delicate silk that skimmed breast and thigh and was slit at the ankle-length hem for ease of movement. There had been sufficient material left for a wide scarf which she intended to drape over her head.

Meanwhile, Yang Fei, tongue between her teeth as she concentrated, swept her red hair into a coronet.

'You look most lovely,' the girl said, patting a last silver headed pin into place. 'The Moon Goddess herself will be jealous of you.'

Lucy, fastening the moonstone necklace about her neck, smiled at the maid with sudden affection.

'You will be going to the feast, won't you?' she asked. 'You and your sister?'

'If it is permitted.' Yang Fei bowed respectfully, her narrow eyes sparkling with excitement. 'The people are holding their own celebrations at the Chi'en Men gate. You will go to the Winter Palace?'

'I suppose so.' Lucy had seen neither Chang Lee nor his father all day.

'I saw the Empress once,' Yang Fei said, pinning the length of black silk round the gleaming coronet of red hair. 'Very far off, with guards about her. They say she knows everything that goes on in Peking.'

'And is amused by most of it,' Lucy rose, small and slim in her black sandals and gazed at her reflection. The scarf softened the vivid hair and in the heart-shaped face the eyes were wide and green.

There was a tap on the door and Chang Lee came in. Lucy saw the little shock of pleasure in his eyes, though his voice was formally polite.

'The litter is come to take you to the Winter Palace. My father and I follow on foot.'

He wore a tunic and trousers of pale yellow with dark red markings at wrist and collar. The sun to her moon, Lucy thought in confusion, and held out her hand to him as they went into the corridor.

'You rival the Moon Goddess tonight,' he said in a low voice as they went down the stairs. 'The Empress hoped for a terrified foreign devil so that our house would lose face, but you look now as if you had belonged in the Forbidden City all your life.'

'I wished to please you, not spite the Empress,' she said, and had no time to enlarge her reply, for Chin Shu was opening the door and the mandarin was bustling them down the steps, past the willow-tree to the street where the red silk-hung litter waited.

They went this time not to the ornate throne-room but to the pleasure gardens that were cunningly concealed within the high walls and paved courtyards of the place. Winding paths, shaded by cherry and plums, meandered between banks of sweet-smelling jasmine. A stream sparkled its course under a series of rustic bridges lit by paper lanterns that cast pools of light over the flower-beds and smooth emerald lawns.

Alighting, Lucy looked about for Chang Lee and saw him striding towards her. The garden was crowded and he exchanged greetings with his acquaintances as he came. One or two people had already bowed smilingly in her direction and she ventured shyly on a Mandarin phrase.

'These are the Harem gardens,' Chang Lee said, taking her arm. 'The royal concubines are kept in the main building over there. They will be watching from behind the lattices.'

Mei-Ling had been destined for the harem. Lucy wished that she were safely behind those latticed windows with plump eunuchs to guard the doors. Then she pushed the thought of the other girl away and smiled up at Chang Lee, deciding that the blend of Oriental and Occidental in his features made him the most attractive man present.

Food was laid out on long tables set in the shadow of a wall, and there were stools at frequent intervals placed next to smaller tables. Servants, clad in the Imperial scarlet, moved about with trays of rice-wine. There was a buzz of high-pitched chatter mingled with the evening throatiness of doves.

'The Empress is not here,' Lucy said, dipping prawns into a spicy sauce. They had taken seats at one of the side tables and Chang Lee was piling her plate.

'Tz'u Hsi likes to make an entrance,' he told her. 'Eat up your food and then we'll go and watch the jugglers.'

'If I eat much more I'll get fat and then you won't love me any more,' she said unthinkingly, and felt the painful colour flush her cheeks as she realised her slip of the tongue.

'You do yourself an injustice,' he began, and something in his tone made her heart leap.

Then two elderly ladies came up and the moment was lost. The newcomers had, it seemed, known Chang Lee since his childhood and seemed bent on a long string of reminiscences, occasionally throwing an English word to Lucy as one might a bone to a puppy.

After a while they moved over to a platform hung with lanterns and watched a troupe of lithe young men and woman perform impossible feats of balancing. The skill of the thin-legged, stick-armed entertainers was breathtaking and she clapped enthusiastically with the rest as, with a final flourish of drums, they formed a quivering pyramid of red and green and lemon.

'They are said to be the best in China,'

said a voice at her elbow.

Stephen Just, black suited and fair haired and looking out of place in this exotic throng, was bowing to her. She looked round for Chang Lee but he had moved away, still talking to the elderly ladies.

'Good evening, Mr Just.'

'Stephen, please. Informality between fellow Britons is to be excused when they are away from home,' he said.

'I begin to feel quite at home,' she said a little stiffly.

'And dress the part? It is quaintly charming, is it not?' He took her arm, steering her through the crowd. 'Are you fully recovered from your unfortunate experience?'

'And most grateful for your kindness,' she said, smiling gratefully even as she wondered how she could have been foolish enough to imagine him attractive. In England he would be considered a most personable young man, but in this setting he looked alien and ill-at-ease.

'I beg your pardon?' She blinked slightly, having missed something he was saying.

'I asked you if you were happily settled with Prince Chang Lee.'

'Indeed I am.' She suspected her voice

was too hearty and rushed on, 'In any marriage there have to be some adjustments on both sides, I imagine.'

'As a bachelor I have to take your word for it. I certainly admire your courage in coming out to a strange land.'

He meant to be kind, but she felt herself bristling under his kindness like a cat whose fur has been stroked the wrong way.

'Courage in staying too,' he went on, heedless of her reaction. 'There will be grave danger very soon for us all, I fear. In my opinion, the women and children should have been sent out of the Legation when they were offered safe conduct, but the ambassador decided to stand firm.'

'The Boxers would never dare to enter the Forbidden City,' she said haughtily.

'One hopes not.' He gave her a sombre look and said, 'If anything were to happen I hope you would not hesitate to call on my aid.'

Lucy mumbled something, wishing he would go away and leave her free to seek out Chang Lee, who was nowhere in sight.

The lanterns were being extinguished, the chattering voices fading to a low humming, the crowd pressing forward silently to the banks of the winding stream. With relief she glimpsed Chang Lee's strong features against the flare of a dying lantern and, murmuring an excuse to Stephen Just, made her way to her husband's side.

'The Empress comes,' he said in a low voice.

There was a soft splashing of water, a rustling as the assembled guests knelt. A sampan, lacquered in red and gold, hung with lotus lanterns, was drifting beneath the arch of the bridge. On a carved chair, high above the black garbed rowers, the Empress sat. A robe of stiff gold brocade covered her from neck to toe, and the black hair was piled up under a crescent head-dress that winked diamonds at the emerging stars. Her face was hidden behind a mask of beaten gold and gold finger-guards protected the long nails on the still shapely hands. Lucy, gaping with the rest, forgot that beneath the splendour was a plump old woman with spiteful eyes, and was stirred by the power and majesty that radiated from that motionless figure.

There was a hush that could almost be tasted and then the Empress lifted her hands, holding them palm upwards. A low wailing of pipes crept from the corners of the darkened garden and lotus blossoms were thrown from the branches of the trees to the surface of the stream. Lucy, glancing up, spotted tiny children moving among the boughs like a new species of bird.

The blossoms floated on the dark water and slowly, like a beautiful woman arising from sleep, the moon rose, round and yellow, from a bank of cloud. The sampan, with its Imperial occupant, was drifting downstream. The lanterns were being rekindled, cups of rice were being passed round, fireworks showering the sky with patterns of red, blue, green, orange and gold.

'The Goddess is in a giving mood,' Chang Lee said. His fingers entwined with Lucy's, and his eyes, dark-shadowed by lamplight, gazed down at her with a question in them. She opened her mouth to reply and heard Stephen Just's precise English tones.

'Ripping good show, wasn't it? The Empress certainly knows how to time her appearances, doesn't she? How are you, Chang Lee?'

'Very well, and you?' Chang Lee had let

her hand drop and was bowing.

Lucy could have wept with frustration. At the instant the moon rose something had leaped between her and Chang Lee and now was swept away by tactless banter.

'Well enough. Surprised to be invited here tonight but Tz'u Hsi believes in playing both ends against the middle. Lucy seems to be thriving. I was just saying to her that if the city is besieged she is welcome to seek refuge at the Legation. I don't suppose the rioters will breach diplomatic immunity.'

'I'd not be too confident of that if I were you,' Chang Lee warned.

'Well, we have stocked up with ammunition and food,' Stephen said cheerfully. 'Water will be the main problem, but we have plenty of champagne.'

'Perhaps it will rain,' Lucy put in brightly.

'And perhaps all the Boxers will turn Christian and crop their pigtails,' Chang Lee said.

He sounded irritated and she wondered if it was with her or with Stephen Just's interruption.

'Of course reinforcements are expected daily,' the young diplomat was saying.

'Let us hope they arrive before the siege begins,' Chang Lee said, moving away.

For a moment Lucy hesitated and then followed him—like a docile Chinese wife, she thought ruefully, but on this night she had no longer felt like a stranger.

The sampan bearing the Empress had gone and the white lotus blossoms were slowly sinking below the moonlit water. In the trees the children giggled and squirmed, eyes wide in their faces. The flutes and pipes and drums still wailed their discordant, strangely hypnotic music and a last firework trailed gold beneath the moon.

'The litter is here, if you wish to go home now,' Chang Lee said, turning to allow her to draw level with him.

'Could we not walk home together?' she asked.

'If you wish. My father will probably use the litter but he's likely to stay longer talking to his friends.'

'Did you wish to stay longer?' she asked.

'The festival has reached its height,' he said. 'I was never one to stay overlong at a party.'

They walked in companionable silence, not touching, through the arched gateways with their massive guards, Lucy, glancing at the heavily muscled men, wondered how many of them were in league with the Boxers, and shivered.

'Are you cold?' Chang Lee asked.

'No, I was wishing that people could live peacefully together,' she said, and he must have caught the wistfulness in her voice, for he took her hand, holding it firmly in his own warm clasp, saying.

'Troubles blow over, even troubles between nations. Will you go into the Legation Compound if we are besieged?'

'I will stay in the House of the Willow,' she said.

'Obstinate and dutiful.' He gave her a fleeting smile as they walked through the narrow streets.

At every corner lanterns hung and fireworks still traced their erratic course across the star-hung sky. It was still warm though the wind had dropped a little, and here and there they passed a little group of merrymakers on their way home from some private celebration.

'Dutiful.' Lucy echoed the word, thinking how dull and flat it sounded. 'Oh, Chang Lee, it is not duty alone that keeps me here.'

'My father's companionship?' He spoke teasingly but there was an underlying seriousness in his voice.

'Your father wishes me to bear you sons,' she said, not daring to look at him. 'I cannot see his wish being fulfilled if you never—never visit me except during the day.'

She had spoken out and her cheeks were flaming. Aunt Harriet would have died of shock if she had heard her niece utter such shameless words.

'Do you think that I have not wished to visit you?' he said. 'I told you that there would be no forcing in this marriage.'

'And Mei-Ling?' They had reached the steps leading up to the willow-tree, and she faced him, her head raised.

'I told you too that she and I have not been together for more than a year. You put up a barrier where none exists.'

Lucy thought of Chen Sula and of Mei-Ling's delicate malice, and shivered again.

'Perhaps I see more clearly than you,' she said in a low voice. 'Old ties of affection can be very strong.'

'And you are jealous?' He said the word on a long breath. 'Dear Lucy, I didn't realise your feeling for me ran so deep. I thought that you and Stephen Just—'

'He admires me,' she said lightly, 'but I find him tedious on closer acquaintance.'

'Come! I have a gift for you.' He took her hand and strode so briskly up the steps that she was hard put to it to keep up with him.

The house was silent, its garlands of white and silver drooping. The servants were evidently at their own celebrations by the Chi'en Men gate.

'Go up to your room while I fetch the gift,' Chang Lee said.

She obeyed, hiding a smile a she mounted the staircase. He had spoken with the authority of a husband and in that lay a subtle reassurance.

Her room had been tidied again, its long windows open to the moonlight. Lucy unpinned the scarf and let loose her long tresses of red hair. Freed from the elaborate chignon they waved over her shoulders, paled by moonglow.

'You look like the Goddess herself,' Chang Lee said, entering the room. 'A slip of a goddess at the moment when she changes from maid to woman.'

'I am a maid still,' she said, and felt a

slow fluttering start up within her as he came to her and, lifting up her hand, slid a gold ring on to her third finger.

'The Chang Lee marriage-ring, worn always by the wife of the eldest son,' he said.

'I am not yet full wife and have no right,' she began, but his arms had encircled her, pulling her tightly against him, his mouth fastening upon her own.

If this was not love she was still content to accept what was offered, to meet his desire with her own hunger, to slake her own thirst in his craving.

The black robe and silky undergarments slithered to her feet and she was clothed in moonstones. Chang Lee had stepped back a pace and was peeling off his own garments. She conquered a sudden shyness and let her gaze wander over the slim golden frame, its muscles taut, the shadows cleaving each limb.

'Come.'

The one word, simply spoken, and then she had placed her hands between his and they moved together out of the moonlight to the shadowed, silk-hung bed.

She had not known it would be like this. She had not realised that pleasure could rise into pain or that pain itself could be exquisite. She had not known herself complete before, nor felt such sweetness in the touch and taste and smell of another body pressing her down into gentle oblivion and rising with her to a fresh wave of sensuous excitement. Chang Lee was an experienced and skilful lover, emptying her mind of all reason, filling her with such a multiplicity of new sensations that she could only rake her nails across his smooth back and cry out softly in words that needed no language learned out of books, for they were held in the secret places of her nature which had stayed sleeping until now.

12

She woke to a bright morning and a tumbled bed. Chang Lee had already risen but the imprint of his head was still on the pillow, and the sheets bore a subtle male scent. So this was marriage! Lucy rolled over on to her back and stretched luxuriously, feeling every muscle tingling with life.

There was a tap on the door and Yang Fei and Yang Chi came in with the breakfast tray and the hot water. From their averted eyes and sly smiles it was clear that the sight of their mistress wearing only a necklace had confirmed whatever rumour they had heard, and it was equally clear from the depths of their bows that in future, as a full wife, she would be treated with even greater courtesy.

'Prince Chang Lee has gone to inspect the forti—' Yang Fei stumbled over the word.

'Fortifications?'

'Yes, if you please. He has been sent also to inspect the roads leading into the city to see if they are still open. In two, three days he will return.'

Lucy felt a momentary exasperation with a husband who could calmly ride off without a word of farewell. Then she reminded herself that he, too, might have been startled by the strength of his own feelings and needed a space in which to accustom himself to the idea of being in love with a foreign devil.

Removing the necklace, she put on the second of the two robes the girls had sewn for her. Cut on the same severe lines its grey-green softened the red of her hair and enhanced her clear skin. After a moment's reflection she took out the dragon brooch the Empress had given her and pinned it to the wide sash.

'The mandarin was called to the court again,' Yang Fei informed her. 'It is said that Prince Su intends to leave the Forbidden City, and that Tz'u Hsi does not wish it.'

'I think that you and I will go down to the gates and find out exactly what is happening,' Lucy decided.

Yang Fei gave a squeak and said imploringly, 'Much safer to stay here and learn Chinese!'

'We can do that this afternoon,' Lucy said firmly. 'Have you a big hat to lend me?'

'A coolie hat?'

'It will match my robe,' Lucy said.

It would also shield her features and, though she had neither the hope nor the intention of passing herself off as Chinese, she would certainly be able to move more freely in a crowd.

Yang Fei, looking exceedingly reluctant, went off to fetch the hat, while Lucy made her way downstairs. Chin Shu came into the hall as she reached the bottom step and bowed, his slanting eyes flicking to her ring.

'The mandarin, Chang Liu, and Prince Chang Lee are absent. Have you any orders for me, princess?' he asked.

Her status had changed. She was no longer a bride, but a full wife with authority over the household when the menfolk were away.

'Please carry on as usual,' she said, hesitating briefly. 'Did you all have a good Moon Feast?'

'Most good, thank you. There was much gaiety.'

'Yang Fei and I are going for a walk,' she continued. 'I will probably be back in time for lunch, but have the cook make something cold in case I'm delayed.'

'You will take care?' he said, with what seemed like genuine anxiety.

'Great care,' she promised, 'but we don't intend to venture very far.'

'Trouble is coming,' he said gravely.

'Perhaps it won't reach us.' She gave him a bright encouraging smile and turned to Yang Fei, who had come in with a wide-brimmed conical hat in her hands.

With the hat tied firmly under her chin, and the maidservant a respectful three paces behind, she stepped out into the courtyard and went down the steps into the narrow street. It was hard to imagine that there was real danger coming closer every day to the high walls that shut out the rest of Peking. Evidence of the previous night's festivities had been cleared away and only cherry and plum blossom decorated the alleys and courtyards. Children, clutching hares and frogs cut out of paper and sacred to the Moon Goddess, were going to school or temple; a red-curtained litter swayed past; white doves circled the pink rooftops, seeking scraps of moon cake left over from the feasting. This, despite its occasional cruelties, was an enchanting city. The chiming of the wind bells, the high voices of the young girls giggling together at a street corner, a brief flash of a dragon kite as it rose into the wind from behind a garden wall—Lucy had never seen the world so clearly before, and each thing upon which her eyes rested seemed bright and delicate.

'It's such a beautiful morning!' she could not help exclaiming to Yang Fei as they walked towards the Ha Ta gate.

'You are happy,' the girl said, dimpling as she smiled back.

'Because I'm in love,' Lucy thought. 'Last night my husband made love to me, and this morning the whole world looks different.'

The high wooden gates that gave an egress from the Forbidden City were barred, but a guard at a narrow side-door let them through, with no more than a cursory glance, into the wider streets beyond.

As before the clamour of Peking burst upon her eardrums with the suddenness of storm, and Lucy paused in bewilderment. Cleaning up had not yet begun in earnest here. There were spent fireworks lying about and a pile of ashes marked the remains of a bonfire. Rickshaws rattled noisily over the cobbles and in the centre of the square a line of men clad in ill-fitting grey uniforms and carrying long staves of bamboo were being drilled by a young man who seemed as uncertain of the correct procedure as his troops were. There were stalls set up here too, but Lucy noticed that the sacks of rice were only half full, the piles of vegetables meagre. Unless the rains came soon, or the Boxers were finally put down, there would be famine.

'Princess Chang Lucy?'

The quiet, cultured voice at her elbow belonged to a tall, elderly man who, despite the heat, wore a padded robe of dark blue. For a moment she was nonplussed but then her brow cleared as she exclaimed.

'It is Lo Kim, is it not?'

She had only seen him in the dim fight of the little pagoda, and she looked at him with interest now, trying to picture him as he must have been twenty years before when he had come to the House of the Willow and met the woman who was to be the inspiration for his greatest artistic creation.

He was still distinguished looking with his narrow features and the black hair coiled in a pigtail on top of his head.

'I apologise for coming to you in the public highway,' he said, 'but it will be the last time we meet, and I would greatly appreciate a few words with you. My house is near if you will honour me by stepping within. Your servant too.'

'I shall be happy to come,' she said, beckoning to Yang Fei to follow as Lo Kim led the way down the street and turned in at a narrow gateway. A tiny courtyard paved in coloured stone adjoined a two-storey wooden house, its roof thatched with bamboo, its tiny windows screened by oiled paper blinds.

'Please to come in.' Lo Kim stooped beneath the lintel of the low doorway.

'Wait for me here.' Lucy indicated a wooden bench to Yang Fei and went into the cool room, bare save for a small cooking-stove, a narrow bed, two stools and a table. A shelf against one wall held a few books and a vase in which a spray of mimosa had been placed.

'My studio is above, but I do less and less work there these days, ' Lo Kim said. 'Please won't you sit down? May I offer you some refreshment?'

'Thank you, no.' Lucy looked round the peaceful room with pleasure. 'This is a charming house.'

'It suits my needs,' he said. 'I have an excellent servant who is worth his weight in gold. Have you been well since we met?'

'Very well.' Lucy brought her gaze back to his face and said, 'You told me this would be the last time we met?'

'I am leaving Peking,' he said. 'In a day or two it will be too late. The riot is becoming a revolution, princess. The Empress will not speak out against the Boxers and it is doubtful if the foreign soldiers will come in time. The way of war was never for me.'

'You're leaving!' Brief as their acquaintanceship had been Lucy felt a sharp regret as if she were losing a friend.

'I am returning to the monastery in the high country,' he said.

'To find the Tao?' She was pleased to have remembered the word.

'Perhaps one never finds it, or perhaps the search is the Tao,' he said, smiling enigmatically. 'And you are happy in your life here? Chang Marie always grieved for her family.'

'I am of the family of Chang Liu,' she said proudly.

'I am happy for you. There has been too much sadness.'

'And the pagoda where the statue lies?' she could not resist asking.

'That is why I am happy to meet you once again. I believe that Chang Liu knows in his heart that his wife was innocent, but he will not hold Ching Ming in her memory.

'I shall hold it for her,' Lucy said.

'I am more grateful than I can say, Princess Chang Lucy. The thought of Chang Marie left alone again held me back from leaving.'

'Will you reach the monastery?' she asked. 'Many of the roads are blocked, I understand.'

'I shall travel light and my servant knows the mountain ways. I shall leave this house and what it contains for any who need shelter. There is nothing of value here, save my books, and those I can hide in my pack. I shall travel with an easier mind now that I know Ching Ming will be kept still for the wife of the mandarin.'

'And I wish you well in your travelling.'

Lucy rose, bowing gravely, her hands clasped together in the manner that seemed quite natural when she wore the Chinese robe.

'It is not wise for Europeans to walk in the open,' he said. 'Please will you not return within the city walls or go to the Legation compound? There are Boxers everywhere, spreading tales of the foreign devils, saying it is they who keep the rain away and bring the hot dust that ruins the rice crops.'

'But that's ridiculous!' she exclaimed.

'When famine threatens people don't think sensibly,' Lo Kim said. 'It would grieve me if sadness came again to the House of the Willow.'

'I shall go back at once,' she promised, bending into the hot sunshine again. Yang Fei rose from the bench where she was seated and waited, her head bent submissively.

'Take care of your mistress, girl,' Lo Kim said to her in English. 'Princess Chang Lucy, it is sad to say farewell to a friend but we part in hope. May you also find the Tao.'

'Lo Kim.' Lucy touched his hand briefly, thinking how strange it was that those long fingers had created such beauty and caused such misery. Then she turned and went into the street again, Yang Fei at her heels.

'We will buy some lychees and then return to the house,' Lucy told her.

'I will buy the lychees if it is your wish,' the girl said, looking anxious. 'Safer for you to go back now. The people murmur against the foreign devils.'

'I'll wait for you here.' Lucy moved into an alcove between two of the wooden houses and stood, hat tugged over her brow. The crowd seemed to have grown larger in the brief period she had spent in Lo Kim's house. There were long strings of people plodding down the dusty road, some riding on mules, others in carts with household goods piled up high. Others were walking, some of them old women with bound feet and patient, wrinkled faces, some of them children with slant-eyed babies strapped to their backs.

There were Boxers running among them, insolent in their red sashes and headbands, curved sabres glinting in their hands. Lucy shrank back, but the men sat their ponies without moving, watching the crowds stream past.

'Lucy! Surely it's Lucy O'Malley!' a voice shrilled.

A woman clad in mantle and flapping sun-hat climbed down from one of the carts and plodded towards her. There was a Chinese baby strapped to her back, but her dust streaked face was a familiar one.

'Mrs Willet?' Lucy hurried to greet her. 'What are you doing here? Where's Mr Willet?'

'Somewhere back there.' Amy Willet flapped a hand vaguely. 'We had to evacuate the Mission at Langchow. We've been on the move for days, coming to the Legation compound. They say that we're going to be under siege. Are you well? For a moment I hardly recognised you in that dress!'

'Oh, I find it more comfortable in the heat,' Lucy said.

'I believe one should keep up appearances,' Amy Willet said, looking faintly disapproving. 'I have insisted on retaining my er—nether garments throughout the journey.'

'I can't understand why the Boxers didn't stop you,' Lucy puzzled. 'Were the roads clear?'

'My dear, the roads are swarming with the barbarians!' the missionary exclaimed. 'It is my firm belief that the rebels have been badly brought up. Oh, they let us through with only insults. I suppose they think that the more are crowded into the Legation the sooner the food and water will run out. That is not fair play, not fair play at all!'

She shook her head, righted her shabby bonnet with a defiant hand, and raised her chin in a tired, gallant little gesture.

'We must move on. When we have settled into our quarters I hope you will come and visit us. Have you made the acquaintance of Stephen Just yet?'

'Indeed I have. He is a friend of my husband,' Lucy said.

'And your husband?' Amy Willet hesitated and said, blushing patchingly, 'I don't wish to pry, but I wondered if you were content.'

'I meant to write to you.'

'I doubt if a letter would have reached me in the present parlous state of affairs,' Amy Willet said. 'My dear, I must hurry. Oh, it will be so pleasant to sit down and enjoy a refreshing cup of tea!'

She waved her hand again and went off, the baby jogging up and down on her back. Lucy gazed after her with affection and then stepped back hastily as a litter hung with yellow silk went past, its bearers kicking up dust in her face. She choked indignantly as the yellow dust stung her eyes and nose, and from within the litter came a high, tinkling cascade of laughter.

Lucy had a momentary glimpse of a parted curtain with slanting eyes mocking her from a delicate face. Then the curtain was dropped again and the litter went by, its occupant hidden again.

'Princess, I have the lychees. Please to

return within the gates now.'

Yang Fei had returned and was tugging at her sleeve. 'That litter? Have you seen it before?' Lucy asked.

'The yellow one? It is one for hire, I think.'

'I see.' Lucy frowned slightly for she was quite certain that it was Mei-Ling who had laughed at her as she stood choking in the dust.

'Please to come.' Yang Fei was evidently nervous of their close proximity to the Boxers. It was a disturbing proof of their confidence that they risked showing themselves openly so near to the walls of the compound and the Forbidden City. The refugees had swelled in number even as Lucy stood there, more and more carts rattling down the winding road past the dried-up paddy-fields.

The gates of the Forbidden City were still barred but the side door stood open still, though the guard studied them closely as they entered. Only those who already lived in Tz'u Hsi's domain were allowed to pass within the Tartar walls. Those who fled from the Boxers would have to cramp themselves into the Legation.

The tranquillity of the city had an

almost unreal beauty as they walked back to the House of the Willow. It was, Lucy thought, as if the world was holding its breath before some threatened catastrophe burst upon it.

The next couple of days went by peacefully. Lucy found a roll of blue cotton in the sewing-room cupboard and set the two maids to making a tunic and trousers for her to wear when the summer reached its height, though what Aunt Harriet would have said if she had known her niece's plans to encase her legs in trousers was something best forgotten!

Lucy herself took the opportunity of venturing into the kitchens again, where she tried out a few words of Mandarin on the giggling servants. At last they seemed to have accepted her presence among them, smiling and bowing and even tugging at her sleeve to draw her attention to the meal they were preparing. She stayed long enough to watch them slice and fry the crisp peppers and aubergines and flake the smoked fish and then went out, heartened by their evident friendliness. Chin Shu came to her once or twice to inquire her wishes about meals and what flowers she wished putting in the various rooms. Lucy guessed that these matters were usually Chen Sula's province, and that the manservant took a sly pleasure in delegating them to her.

The housekeeper came and went silently, answering only when she was directly addressed. Once or twice Lucy saw her plump figure coming back across the courtyard, evidently returning from a visit to her daughter, and once Lucy saw the little boy, Tong Su, on the fringe of the orchard. She wondered if he had been ordered to keep away from the big house and felt a sudden sympathy for the child. It was not his fault that he had been born, and she could understand Chang Lee's affection for his small son and even his determination not to abandon his youthful mistress.

'Being loved has made me a much nicer person,' she said aloud to her reflection in the mirror as she dried herself after her bath one evening. Then her brow clouded a little. Chang Lee had made love to her, but perhaps that was not the same as loving her. He had been away for three days and she craved the reassurance of his presence.

There was the rattle of the door handle

and she reached for her robe and was belting it around herself when Chang Lee himself walked in. To see him just as she was thinking about him struck her as a delightful coincidence and, abandoning formality, she ran to greet him. His embrace was warm, his mouth hungry upon her own, but when she leaned away from him a little she saw that his expression was preoccupied.

'Is the news bad?' she asked.

'As bad as it can be,' he said sombrely. 'The supply routes are completely blocked by the rebels and the peasants in the outlying villages too terrified of reprisals to take up arms against them.'

'I saw the people coming to the Legation compound,' Lucy said. 'So many of them, and Boxers openly in the crowd watching and sneering. I saw Mrs Willet, the missionary's wife. They had fled from the Mission at Langchow.'

'They were fortunate,' he said gravely. 'Many missionaries have ended up recently with their heads on poles!'

'But the army—,' she began.

'Untrained and undisciplined. The Imperial Guard will only take orders directly from the Empress and Tz'u Hsi will do nothing but sit on the dragon throne looking enigmatic!'

'So they will besiege the city?' She spoke in a low voice, a frown creasing her brow.

'The gates were shut at sundown today,' Chang Lee said. 'Oh, it is still possible for those within the walls to risk venturing out but no more will be admitted to the compound. There simply isn't room for those who are packed there already.'

'Will the European soldiers get here?' she enquired anxiously.

'Rumour contradicts rumour and nobody knows anything.' He broke off, staring at her. 'You said European soldiers as if you were Chinese,' he said slowly.

'I feel at home here,' she said simply. 'I am of the family of Chang now.'

'And my wife.' He drew her close again, slipping his hands beneath her robe, his lean frame straining against her. A low moan rose from her throat and her eyes closed as she wound her fingers in his black hair.

His look of tiredness had gone and there was desire in the black eyes that pierced her own. She felt herself lifted and laid down upon the bed, her hair spread upon the pillow, her robe opened. His lips moved over the contours of her body, his hands stroked her into an eager and quivering submission. She arched to meet him and was again complete.

'What was that?' Dimly, as the haze of pleasure receded, Lucy heard a far off noise like surf beating against cliffs, 'I'm not sure.' Chang Lee rose, reaching for his clothes and pulling them on.

Lucy pulled her own garment close and joined him, as he stepped on to the balcony. In the courtyard several of the servants had gathered, chattering shrilly and pointing into the sky where golden flares streaked up towards the emerging moon.

'Is it fireworks?' Lucy heard herself ask childishly, and heard his sombre reply as he drew her close to his side.

'It is the siege, my love. The Legation compound is being fired upon.'

13

The siege had begun. Lucy, if she had ever considered it at all, had always imagined that a besieged city would be a place of confused and despairing excitement, but life in the Forbidden City seemed to continue its tranquil, unchanging tenor. Certainly the nights were lit up by the sinister flares and the rattle of artillery sounded clearly through the still air, but in the streets the trees dripped fragrant blossom over the paving-stones and the laughter of children mingled with the cooing of doves. The gates were barred and bolted now, and anyone venturing out had to take with them a yellow token issued by the guard to identify them when they wished to return.

The Boxers were camped about the walls of the Legation, occasionally sallying forth to fire at the men keeping watch on the high parapet. From the balcony of her room Lucy could see the glow of the rebels' bonfires against the evening sky and hear very faintly the clashing of steel as they practised their sword drill.

'Princess Chang Lucy, I have asked the master for leave of absence,' Chen Sula said abruptly as Lucy was coming out of the library one afternoon.

It was the first time the housekeeper had addressed her for many days, and Lucy frowned slightly, wondering what had induced this sudden announcement.

'My daughter, Mei-Ling, is alone in her house except for the child and the old servant,' Chen Sula continued. 'She is nervous of the Boxers and wishes for company until the danger is over.'

'Yes, of course you must go.' Lucy forced herself to speak warmly. She was enjoying Chang Lee's presence so much that she could afford to spare a generous thought for the woman who had borne his child and still probably cared deeply for him.

'If I am needed,' Chen Sula said, 'I am quickly to be found.'

'Yes.' Lucy nodded, unable to repress a little smile of relief.

The silent comings and goings of that plump figure, the watchful stare of those inimical black eyes, had troubled her more than she would admit.

It was a pleasure when Chen Sula had gone, to be able to move freely about the large house without the fear of turning a corner and coming upon that watching figure. Lucy had explored all the rooms now, though out of politeness she only gave a cursory glance into the other bedrooms, noting that Chen Sula's apartment was as bare as if she had no intention of ever returning and that the mandarin's bedroom was even more opulently furnished than her own. Chang Lee came to her nearly every night, sometimes holding her closely and talking to her softly until she fell asleep, sometimes impatient to satisfy their mutual hunger. His lovemaking on these occasions was swift and passionate, stirring her into an answering flame. Yet there was a subtle sweetness about the hours when they lay together while he talked of various matters, touching lightly on one topic and then another, leading her on to relate anecdotes of Aunt Harriet.

'When all this is over we must bring her out to stay with us,' he said.

'I cannot imagine what she would make of China,' Lucy confided.

'Nor of what China would make of your

Aunt Harriet,' Chang Lee said, muffling laughter against her shoulder.

It was safe to talk of Aunt Harriet, to plan for her visit, to practise her small fund of Mandarin. There were still some subjects that she hesitated to raise. The name of Mei-Ling hung, unspoken, between them. Lucy was almost certain that Chang Lee no longer visited his former mistress and, while she could not regret it, she sometimes thought of the little black-haired boy. Tong Su ought not to be completely separated from his father, but she could see no way of achieving that unless she admitted Mei-Ling into her life and she was not prepared to do that.

'What is the Empress going to do?' she asked, turning her thoughts into a less sensitive path.

'Nobody has the slightest idea what the Empress is going to do.' Chang Lee rolled over to his stomach, propping his chin on his hands. 'It's my personal opinion that she is beginning to lose her grasp of affairs. Intrigue turns upon itself in the end, and the serpent bites its own tail. Did you ever visit your missionary friend?'

'No. No, I didn't.' Lucy spoke quietly, for she had meant to go to the Legation compound and neglected to do so.

'I won't mind,' Chang Lee said, amusement in his voice, 'if you do run into the estimable Mr Just. He and I are good friends underneath our surface differences. Stephen believes that the English were born to civilise the Chinese and I believe the Chinese way of life ought not to be lightly tossed aside. One thing we do have in common is our mutual admiration for a certain red-haired foreign devil.'

He reached for her hand, kissing the palm and folding her fingers over the caress. His head, raised from the pillow, was sharp edged in the moonlight and the lock of black hair tumbling over his brow gave him a curiously vulnerable look. She was reminded suddenly of Tong Su and pulled Chang Lee down to her, shutting out her thoughts in the warmth of their shared passion.

The next day was like the days that had gone before, with the same hot wind sweeping the streets, the same air of peaceful unreality. Chang Lee had shared her breakfast instead of returning to his own room, and then gone with his father to the Winter Palace where the Empress was holding another of the series of Council meetings at which nothing was ever decided. Lucy wandered about, feeling a trifle lost. Yang Fei was busy with the making of the blue tunic and trousers and Lucy had postponed her lesson in Chinese. She went briefly into the kitchen to inquire of Chin Shu what had been planned for luncheon and the evening meal, and then wandered off into the big reception apartment where the ivory girl leaned out of the willow tree. This beautiful apartment needed people to admire the rich colours of floor and walls, and sit at the tables. When the rebellion was over she would try to persuade Chang Lee to invite guests here to fill the empty space with friends and laughter, and to turn the shame of a foreign wife into the pride of a gracious hostess who had adapted herself to a new land.

Abruptly, without knowing why, she remembered the words of the soothsayer as he had bent over the scattered yarrow sticks.

'You stand alone in a place of danger. Enemies. Many tears. On the night of the willow a flower will grow from the withered trunk and your weakness will become strength.'

The words made no sense but they frightened her, and she turned thankfully as Chang Lee's voice called her from the hall. She ran to meet him, her face lifted for his kiss, and the words of the soothsayer slid out of her memory.

'We'll have a quick meal and then I'll take you to see your friend,' he said.

'She's not exactly my friend,' Lucy began doubtfully, but he shook his head at her in mock severity.

'She took care of you when you were travelling here, my love, and you must pay your respects to her. Put on your English dress. Your friend will not be happy to see you in native dress.'

To her surprise she was really reluctant to change into the tight corset and cramping bodice of her lace dress. Even her hat with its froth of veiling, felt cumbersome after the shady coolie hat. She came downstairs, scowling at him, lifting her skirt irritably.

'Now you're an English lady again,' Chang Lee said lightly, holding her at arm's length. 'Come, we'll take the short cut through the inner door to save risking your pretty person in the open streets beyond the walls.'

'I didn't know there was a short cut,' Lucy said in surprise.

'There are several back entrances from the Forbidden City into the Legation compound,' he told her. 'The Empress believes in keeping a close watch on diplomatic affairs!'

'Then why don't the Europeans come into the Forbidden City?' she asked, puzzled.

'For the same reason that Christians don't stroll into Mecca,' he said. 'The penalty for trespass is death and there is no diplomatic immunity in Tz'u Hsi's domain.'

There was a grimness to the set of his mouth as if, with each day that passed, his sympathy for the Empress was dwindling. Lucy hoped that his changing attitude was partly due to her own readiness to be his full wife, and her smile at him was a hopeful one.

'And I give you permission to be charming to Stephen Just,' he said, as they walked down the steps.

'While you flirt with Amy Willet?' She slanted him a smiling glance.

'I cannot stay for a long visit,' he said disappointingly. 'I am due to inspect a detatchment of volunteer soldiers this afternoon.'

'Reinforcements? So you think the Forbidden City will really be attacked?'

'I think it is likely, and the guards are under strength. I'll call back for you at dusk.'

He had turned into a narrow side street with a door set into the wall at the end. A young soldier lounged by it, picking his teeth and looking bored, but he sprang to attention as Chang Lee spoke to him sharply.

They passed through into a stone summer-house which opened into a crowded street. Lucy recognised the building where Stephen Just had given her lunch, but the courtyard beyond which had been empty on that occasion was now filled with wooden huts and canvas awnings beneath which people were moving about, some stirring rice in large cauldrons that hung over smoking charcoal fires, others nursing babies or gazing blankly ahead of them.

'Mission Chinese,' Chang Lee said, nodding towards them. 'They have as much reason as the Europeans to fear the Boxers. Your Mrs Willet will be in the British Legation.'

Mrs Willet was indeed where she was expected, and hurried to greet them, her face no longer dusty but still drawn with anxiety.

'My dear, I have been wondering how to get a message to you,' she said in a rush. 'We are so short of supplies here that I hoped it might be possible for you to help out. There are so many children here who require milk and fruit, and the doctors are running out of medicines. Oh, you must be dear Lucy's husband! I do beg your pardon for not realising—it is Your Highness, is it not? And I suppose that I ought to address Lucy as—it is difficult to think clearly on such matters! Since we arrived from Langchow we have been in complete confusion.'

'You must call me Chang Lee,' he said, taking her hand before she could attempt a curtsy. 'I will see what I can do about having some fruit brought in for the children, but the medicines are in short supply everywhere, I'm afraid. Have you comfortable quarters?'

'I'm sharing a room with three other ladies,' Amy Willet said, pushing her greying hair back from her forehead. 'Really we are most fortunate. So many Chinese refugees are sleeping in the streets in those makeshift tents. I do wish the Empress would help to relieve the overcrowding by admitting some into the Forbidden City.'

'The Empress wants you to be overcrowded,' Lucy said tightly. 'She thinks it will rid China of foreigners more quickly if they can be starved out or hit by some disease or other.'

'It is the latter which I fear,' Amy Willet said, wringing her hands gently. 'All these people crammed together in one place and such a shortage of water. The wells are beginning to run dry, you know, and the rice supplies have diminished to a mere trickle. I fear typhus and dysentery will break out soon among the children. But I haven't offered you tea! Do forgive my bad manners. We still have a small stock—but most people are quenching their thirst with champagne! Joseph and I have always been total abstainers, of course, but one should be prepared to drop a principle in cases of extreme necessity.'

'How is Mr Willet?' Lucy cut into the flow.

'Helping in the hospital. He is hoping to organise Bible classes, but the people are so feckless that it is difficult to get them together in the same place at the same time. But you must come and have some tea, my dear Lucy. I want so much to hear about the wedding.'

'It was—a proxy marriage,' Lucy said, flushing.

'Oh? Oh, how nice!' Amy Willet gave a vague, slightly bewildered smile.

'Lucy, I have to go now,' Chang Lee said. 'Why don't you have Mrs Willet help you draw up a list of urgently needed supplies and I will see if anything can be done. I'll return for you later. Mrs Willet, it has been a pleasure to meet you. Lucy.'

He clasped her hands warmly between his own, bowed, and strode away.

'My dear, what a charming young man!' Amy Willet exclaimed, gazing after him. 'He looks almost European.'

'His mother was a French lady,' Lucy explained, 'and he was educated in England.'

'He is certainly very handsome and you look most prosperous. I am so glad to find you content. Joseph and I feared that the prince might be ugly or unpleasant. Shall we go and sit down? To tell you the truth I shall be glad to take the weight off my feet for an hour. I am beginning to think I am not as young as I was.'

Soon the two ladies were seated in an alcove, cups of fragrant tea before them, the noises from the courtyard muted by the closed door.

'Peking is such a busy place,' Amy Willet sighed. 'Our Mission at Langchow was a haven of peace in comparison, but I suppose those dreadful Boxers are occupying it now. They say the Empress is secretly in league with them.'

'I can believe anything of Tz'u Hsi,' Lucy said feelingly. 'When I saw her—'

'You've seen her! What is she like?' the other interrupted eagerly.

'Sinister and magnificent,' Lucy said slowly. 'She's a fat old woman really, but in her robes and jewels she has a kind of barbaric splendour. She admires courage, I think, but she's a natural bully who tramples on gentleness and exploits weakness. We went to the Festival of the Moon Goddess, and she was there on a high seat in a boat that was rowed down the river. In the throne-room the arms of her chair are carved dragon heads of jade, with ruby eyes.'

'One's soul ought to be above such

matters,' Amy Willet said, 'but it does sound very luxurious! And your own house, my dear. The mandarin's, I should say. Is it a palace?'

'Not quite, but it's very large.' Lucy launched into a description of its rooms, her account carefully pruned of all reference to Mei-Ling or Tong Su. She talked instead of the lessons she was taking from Yang Fei, of the well-stocked library, of her journey from Tientsin when the wagon had been intercepted by Boxers.

The afternoon passed pleasantly, only the occasional crack of a rifle reminding them that, despite the surface inactivity, this was still a city under siege. The Europeans and their Chinese converts were penned up here as helpless as animals in a trap, and would be in dire straits if the promised reinforcements didn't arrive soon.

There was still no sign of Chang Lee and, despite Amy Willet's obvious pleasure in their long conversation, it was clear that she was anxious to return to her duties. At last, intercepting her hostess's surreptitious glance at the clock on the wall, Lucy rose, carefully folding the list of supplies with which Amy Willet had provided her.

'I'm afraid my husband has been delayed. I will make my own way back, but if he comes, will you tell him?'

'My dear, you're not venturing beyond the walls!' Amy Willet said in alarm.

'We came by a private door,' Lucy said.

'I have heard that there are entrances into the Forbidden City,' Amy Willet said, lowering her voice slightly. 'Not that I would ever dare to trespass. It is a constant worry to me that one of the children might wander through, for I dread to think what might happen to them.'

'Nothing very much. The Empress is said to be fond of children.'

'But of European children?' The older woman looked doubtful.

'Give my regards to Mr Willet and to Stephen Just,' Lucy said, drawing on her gloves. 'I am sorry to have missed them.'

'Mr Just is taking his turn at patrolling the walls,' Amy Willet said, going with her to the door. 'The Boxers shout up insults and hurl firecrackers over, but our great fear is that they will bring up scaling ladders and extra guns. Joseph says that our own supply of ammunition is getting very low. Not that he approves of fighting, of course but they seem to have done a great deal of it in the Bible.'

Her anxious face and voice stayed with Lucy as she turned into the narrow passage leading to the door in the wall. To her relief the same soldier was on duty, looking even more bored than before. He seemed to recognise her however, and let her through silently. After the heat and noise of the compound the streets were quiet and comparatively cool, the scorching wind tempered by a soft, yellow sunset and the canopies of peach and almond trees that overhung the pavements. She passed the gate below Mei-Ling's house and came to the long wall that ran along the side of the orchard. There was a door set into the wall, easy to miss because its surface was painted the same pinky-red as the stone. This was the door through which Lo Kim had slipped, on his way to pay tribute to the memory of Chang Marie.

On impulse Lucy pushed it open and stepped within. She saw at once that she stood in a narrow path between the wall and the back of the pagoda. There was thick moss under her feet and the trees arched fruit laden boughs above her. When she had first come to the House of the Willow the trees had been blossom-decked, but now many of them bore fruit. She would persuade Chang Lee to send some to the compound.

As if the thought of him conjured his presence, his voice sounded close at hand. She opened her mouth to call, and stopped, tilting her head to listen. His deeper tone had been joined by a light, silvery voice speaking in Chinese.

She knew the voice even before she glimpsed the slender form through the trees, who talked with Chang Lee. Mei-Ling seemed to be angry. Lucy could discern a shrillness in her voice, an impatience in the shrug of her narrow shoulders as she turned away. Chang Lee stepped into view, reaching for her hand, his own voice pleading.

They spoke in Chinese, too quickly for Lucy to follow with her own limited knowledge of the language, but there was no mistaking the fact that he asked and Mei-Ling refused. So his lovemaking had been nothing more than a skilled attempt to make his foreign wife content. He had never intended to give up his former mistress at all, but it looked as if Mei-Ling had as little intention as Lucy of sharing him.

Rage and desolation seized her and she took a step forward with no thought in her mind but to confront them. Then something tapped her sharply on the head. She felt the impact of it even through her hat, and then a great blackness engulfed her and the scorching wind rushed through the numbed spaces of her brain.

There were noises somewhere. Dim, cracking noises and voices that came and went, and blurred into darkness. She was being rocked in a swing that flew higher and higher, Chang Lee pushing it from one side and Mei-Ling pushing it from the other. The swing came down with a bump, jarring her bones.

Lucy struggled against a feeling of intense dizziness. It was dark and so hot it was difficult to breathe properly. Her head seemed to be dangling down, but when she tried to move it her temples were stabbed by flashing pain, and her fingers, scrabbling helplessly, met coarse-fibred material. Sacking! She was in a sack. Lucy felt an irrational pleasure in having worked that out, and let out a cry as her whole body was jolted violently from side to side.

The voices came closer and then faded away, and the blackness came down again. Lucy heard the whinnying of a horse and thought, as she slid into oblivion, that it was most unladylike to travel in a sack, tied over the back of a pony.

She opened her eyes to grey light, filtering through a shuttered window. There was a mattress beneath her and her mouth felt as if it had been scraped with a pan scourer. At least she could breathe freely, though when she rolled over her head ached abominably. There was a large mug on the wooden floor near to her hand. Lucy struggled up to her elbow and drank greedily, water splashing the front of her dress as her hand slopped some of the contents.

At last her throat was less parched and her head a little clearer. She dragged herself into a sitting position, gasping as the dull ache in her temples sharpened into agony again. She was in a small room, bare save for the mattress on which she crouched, and a bucket in the corner. Her hat, its tulle torn and its crown bent was in another corner, looking as if someone had flung it there in disgust. Her hair had come loose from its pins and tumbled in long red locks over her shoulders. If Chang Lee could see her now he would certainly think her unattractive. Then she remembered that Chang Lee had made an excuse to leave her at the Legation and gone to meet Mei-Ling, and tears rushed into her eyes.

The door at the other side of the room opened, and her tears were stayed before they had begun to fall.

The man who lounged in and stood, grinning down at her, was the big shaven-headed Boxer who had watched his men fight for the coins that Chin Shu had thrown for them on the way to the Forbidden City. Now he watched her with the same malicious amusement, his little eyes squinting in the broad expanse of his face. There was a dagger stuck through his red sash and his pigtail was tied with red ribbon. There was something so incongruous in that bow of gay silk that Lucy fought back a hysterical desire to laugh. Instead she compressed her lips, ignoring the pounding of her head, and said loudly, in Chinese.

'Get out!'

The Boxer evidently understood her. She fancied a faint surprise in his face before he opened the door and went. A bolt was rammed into its socket and then there was silence again.

14

The grey light faded into blackness and Lucy fell into the sleep of exhaustion, waking to the brilliant sunlight that pierced the shutters and striped the mattress on which she lay. Her head still ached if she moved quickly and her joints were stiff after the jolting ride, but she was ravenously hungry.

She was also becoming extremely angry. The Boxers must have been hiding in the orchard when she had let herself in through the side door. It was surprising they hadn't killed her at once, but clearly she was more valuable to them alive. Perhaps they were holding her for ransom. If so, then she wondered how much Chang Lee would be prepared to pay. Perhaps he would be relieved to have her taken so that Mei-Ling had no further cause for jealousy. Hastily Lucy began to think about the Boxers. It was better to feel angry than to be completely and utterly miserable.

The bolt was pulled back and the Boxer came in again. Lucy scrambled to her feet and stood with her back against the wall. In such a situation the only thing to do was to attack, and she spoke loudly and slowly in Mandarin, rapping out each word.

'Food! Water! Clean clothes!'

As before he looked surprised. Then he nodded and went out. He was gone for such a long time that she feared he was never going to return, but eventually the door opened and two women came in. Lucy, staring at them, recognised them as the ones who had served her meal in the inn on her way to the Forbidden City. She must be in the hostelry on the road to Tientsin. The women put down what they carried and scuttled out again without looking at her.

There was a bowl of rice with bits of meat in it, a mug of water, some lychees, another larger bowl of water with a small towel, and some clothing folded neatly. So her instinct had been right. She was not to be killed but to be kept for some other purpose.

The meal was a satisfying one and she ate hungrily before washing the worst of the dirt off herself. The clothes consisted of a faded blue tunic and trousers such as the peasants wore, carefully patched and mended but clean. Lucy wriggled out of her ruined dress and corset with relief and put on the unfamiliar garments. Her comb and a few coins were in the pocket of the discarded dress and when she drew them out the list of supplies came with them. As she combed the tangles out of her hair and braided it into a pigtail she began to plan as coldly and carefully as her perturbed state of mind would allow.

The younger of the two women returned to take away the empty bowls and, this time, paused within the half-closed door to stare at Lucy. Perhaps the garments made her seem less like a foreign devil for the girl joined her hands and gave the customary bow of greeting.

'For you.' Lucy spoke in Mandarin, lowering her voice for fear of listeners, and pressing a coin wrapped in the supply list in her hand with her other hand she put her finger to her lips, enjoining silence.

The girl nodded, sudden intelligence in her face and bent to collect the bowls and the discarded dress. Then she went out again, leaving Lucy more hopeful than she had been for some time. It was a hope that was to rise up and then flicker in the days that followed. Three times a day one or other of the women came in with food and water for washing and drinking, and twice the huge Boxer lounged in to grin at her mockingly, his little eyes sliding over her in a way that made Lucy suddenly cold with terror.

Only the sunsets, glimpsed through the slatted blinds, gave her an indication of the days that passed. By now the sunsets had numbered five, but she felt she had been in the room for ever, had paced every inch of its floor, learned by heart every mark on its walls. There was nothing to do but think and her thoughts were bitter ones. By now the ransom would surely have been demanded and she was beginning to believe that Chang Lee had abandoned her to her fate. In due course a letter would be sent to Aunt Harriet, telling her of the sad news of her niece's death in the Boxer Rising. She would be like Chang Marie with nobody to keep Ching Ming for her.

Lucy wept softly, wishing she had never come to China, never fallen in love with Chang Lee, never tried to make him love her in return.

Her tears splashed down the side of her nose, spotting her tunic. 'Many tears,' the soothsayer had said, and she remembered the pattering of the yarrow sticks on the table. The pattering now was above her head and she raised it sharply, listening. Rain! Rain was stinging the bamboo roof, showering fine needles down to the dusty road. Impatiently she scrubbed her cheeks dry and went over to the window, hope raising again. The rain meant fresh water for the compound, fresh water for the paddy-fields. Something would surely begin to change now.

As if the rain were a signal the door opened and the Boxer appeared, jerking his head and saying 'Come' in an abrupt manner that made Lucy's temper rise.

She followed him meekly, however, into the big, main room of the inn. There were half a dozen other Boxers lounging round the stove. There was a dead silence as Lucy entered and two of the men drew away, making the sign against the evil eye. The small proof of fear gave her confidence and she stopped dead, scowling, raising her voice in what she hoped was a tone of authority.

'Do you speak English?'

'I speak it,' the Boxer said, lowering his bulk to a table that creaked alarmingly under his weight.

'Then I demand to know why I am being held,' she rushed on. 'I demand to know by what right you abducted me and brought me here! I am Princess Chang Lucy of the house of the mandarin, Chang Liu.'

'I know that,' he said flatly.

'And when the mandarin finds out what you have done you will be punished,' she said, her assumed anger becoming real. 'You will have your head cut off for daring to carry me away by force. The Empress Tz'u Hsi—'

'It is Mei-Ling I please, not Tz'u Hsi,' he said.

'Oh.' The anger drained out of her and she sat down abruptly, her knees suddenly quaking.

'Mei-Ling tells me to take the foreign devil away, hold her until the bandit Ting Ha comes.'

'Ting Ha?'

'Big Bandit man. Very powerful. He comes to buy slaves from the Boxers.'

'A slave!'

'Good money for a foreign devil slave,' the Boxer grinned. 'Perhaps he will sell you to another master or keep you for himself. Any day now he comes.'

'And Mei-Ling told you to do this?' Lucy's voice had faded to a whisper.

'Mei-Ling and I are lovers now,' he said. 'She is weary of Chang Lee, weary of her house. Chang Lee discovers that Mei-Ling is seeing Boxer chief and he pleaded with her not to do such a bad thing, and Mei-Ling will not answer.'

It was clear to her now. Chang Lee had not been begging Mei-Ling to take him back. He had been trying to persuade her to give up her Boxer lover. There was no ransom demanded. Mei-Ling had simply used her lover to carry out her own private revenge against the foreign wife who had supplanted her in the arms of the man she no longer loved. Chang Lee would assume that Lucy had disappeared, and though she was certain now that he would seek her it was almost equally certain that the bandit chief would arrive first. Lucy didn't like to think about what would happen then.

'You will bring good price,' the Boxer said, grinning again. 'I will have money and Mei-Ling will be my wife.'

'You will need me to be in good health,' she said, setting her chin firmly and controlling her shaking. 'In that room I will get sick and die, I need fresh air, exercise. Your Ting Ha won't pay good money for a dead slave!'

He frowned, pulling at his lower lip, and one of the other men called to him from across the room, and the others laughed, evidently at some coarse pleasantry.

Their leader ignored them, speaking to her again in the loud, bullying tone that put her nerves on edge.

'You sleep in there. Spend day out here. Walk outside with man to watch you.'

'While you sit about here and grow fat? Are you afraid of the foreign devil soldiers that you don't fight?' she taunted. 'Is the rising over then, and the Boxers whipped away?'

'My men and I return to the city,' he said. 'There is much fighting there now. Burning and killing. My men and I return, but we leave a guard—two guards with you. In one week we come back. Ting Ha will come then.'

A moment before he had said the bandit chief would arrive any day. Probably he had no definite idea when the transaction would be made. It was a crumb of comfort to hold on to. In a week many things could happen. The reinforcements might arrive, or Chang Lee discover where she was. Lucy refused to consider the possibility that the Legation might be stormed or Chang Lee killed.

The Boxers moved away as she went over to the stove to warm herself. That, too, was a point in her favour, for it meant that the guard assigned to her might not get too close and through the open door Lucy had already glimpsed the line of sturdy-legged horses waiting patiently in the rain. As she held her hands over the glowing coals she felt hope spring up in her again. Whatever happened now she knew that Chang Lee had been speaking the truth when he told her that he and Mei-Ling had not been lovers for more than a year. His visits to her had been to see his son and to try to persuade her to give up her Boxer lover. Whatever happened she had that to console her.

It was infinitely better to be allowed into the main part of the inn instead of being cramped in the little room. During the next few days Lucy devoted herself, as far as possible, to merging into the background. The inn had evidently been taken over by the rebels and, apart from the two women, she saw no sign of any local people. They had probably run away before the Boxers came and the rain-soaked paddy-fields were deserted. Lucy spent her time either sitting by the window watching the dripping landscape or helping the two Chinese women with their small household tasks. At first they had seemed reluctant to let her near the cooking pots or the willow brooms with which they swept the floors, but she had insisted silently on helping, even forcing herself to lay meals before the men who sprawled at the table. One of them reached up on one occasion and seized the end of her plait, tugging her head near to his own. Their leader had sprang up from his own place, his hand on the hilt of his dagger, and hissed something so obviously threatening that the other released her at once and cowered away, scowling. It was clear that she was not to be physically molested, and Lucy guessed that it was not out of any sense of honour or compassion but simply because her value as a slave would drop if she had been raped.

Once or twice a day, a coolie hat protecting her from the emptying skies, she went outside the long wooden building and trudged through the mud, followed by one or other of the men, the temptation to take to her heels and run was sometimes very strong, but it would have been mere wasted effort, so she walked slowly, contriving each time to move a little nearer to the horses.

On the third day she woke to find half the horses gone along with their masters, and a small kitchen-knife tucked into the towel that the girl brought with the water for washing.

Lucy put the knife in the pocket of her tunic and went out to the main room. There were three or four Boxers still round the table and they looked up as she walked in, but the big, shaven-headed one had evidently gone with the others. It was still raining but the sky was brightening slightly as a feeble sun struggled through.

She took her own bowl of rice and chopped eggs over to the door and sat, eating it, and gazing over the churned expanse of yellowish mud. They were no more than a few hours' ride from Peking, but for all the information she had concerning the siege she might as well have been back in Oldham.

There were riders coming up the road. She set aside the bowl and stood up, straining her eyes towards them. One of the men within came up and pushed past her into the open, calling out a greeting. For an instant Lucy's heart sank as she spotted the bright red headscarves and sashes of the newcomers and then, without thinking about the risk of what she was doing, she sped through the open door and ran towards the horses, the mud sucking at her shoes.

The ponies were tethered to a long rope and they were unsaddled. In the back of her head Aunt Harriet's voice sounded quite plainly. 'You must be clean daft, Lucy Mary O'Malley. You've never ridden a horse in your life!'

Then she was sawing at the rope with her sharp little, knife, and scrambling up to the back of one of the ponies, hooking her leg over the broad back and clutching frantically at its coarse mane.

There were shouts, and men running, and mud splashing up, and the rain blowing into her face. A shot whistled over her head and she gasped out, ducking instinctively. The pony was moving, but at an ambling gait which suggested it was out for an afternoon stroll. Lucy drummed her heels frantically against the beast's sides, hearing her own frustrated sobbing below the shouts and clashing of swords. Another shot cracked through the rain, and a blur of red flashed at the edge of her vision.

She struck out blindly with her fists, but she was being lifted from her horse and a voice she scarcely recognised in her panic said.

'Be still and hang on!'

Chang Lee, a red scarf wound round his head, was holding her tightly on his own horse and firing a pistol at those who pursued. His companions circled round them, and she saw Chin Shu's long face, dirtied and yet as calm as if he were inquiring what she would like for luncheon.

Lucy clung on until her fingers ached, and closed her eyes against the rain and wind. They were galloping along the road and the shouting was growing fainter.

The paddy-fields were seen dimly like the landscape of a dream. In a moment she would wake up and find out that China was a yellow splodge in a geography book.

The world slowed and steadied, and was still real. Chang Lee pulled the horse to a standstill and made her more comfortable on the saddle in front of him.

'You found me,' she said, and began to cry and laugh at the same time.

'The girl at the inn gave her soldier sweetheart the list of supplies and he had the wit to bring it to the Legation. Lord knows how he got through the Boxer lines, but he did so. Stephen Just gave it to Amy Willet and she sent a message to me. I was out of my mind with worry.'

'It was Mei-Ling,' she said breathlessly. 'She and her lover! Why didn't you tell me?'

'I hoped to persuade her to make a respectable marriage,' he said, clicking his tongue to the horse to make it start up again. 'She would take no advice from me, and in a way I can't blame her. What was between us is dead now and she has the right to make her own choice. But she was a fool to take up with a rebel and a criminal to have you snatched away in such a fashion!'

'It doesn't matter, now that you are here,' she said, thankful for the hard strength of his encircling arms. 'Nothing matters now that you're here!'

'We must get back to the city,' he said, gesturing to the others to follow him. 'The fighting is bitter now. I hoped the rain might help a little, but the rebels press harder. The walls of the Legation compound have already been breached in several places and many buildings set on fire. Keep your head down and hang on, for we must ride fast now, and there's no telling what trouble will meet us along the road.'

She obeyed meekly, closing her eyes tightly as the road dipped and swayed under the threshing hoofs. In a day or two her limbs would ache intolerably, but there was no time to think of anything beyond the necessity of holding on as they thundered towards the increasing din of guns and firecrackers.

The walls of the Legation compound were still manned. Chang Lee pulled off his red scarf and rode in through a gap in the stone, pulling her from the saddle and shouting impatiently to a young marine who stood gaping at him.

'Get this lady to Amy Willet's house.'

'I'm staying with you,' Lucy began.

'My love, there's a small war going on,' he said, laughter softening the grimness of his tone. 'Go to Amy Willet now. I have my volunteer Chinese to command.'

The marine, coming to life, had snapped to attention, his startled gaze flying to her mud-spattered figure, the long braid of red hair soaked dark with rain.

'Stay with Amy Willet,' Chang Lee said again and then was gone, weaving and ducking through the crowd milling in the compound. The marine took Lucy's arm and ran with her along the side of the wall into a narrow street where stretchers were being rushed through the rain into the Legation hospital.

'Mrs Willet is helping out there, ma'am,' the marine said. 'You'll pardon me if I get back on duty now?' He saluted and hurried back into the main square.

'Lucy! My dear child, I am so happy to see you safe!' Amy Williet dropped a pile of bandages she was rolling and flew across the ward. 'We have been in the most fearful anxiety about you, and then Chang Lee—he insists I call him so—rode off to rescue you. I was sadly lacking in faith, for I was quite certain that he would be murdered on the way, but the mandarin was certain that events would fall out well.'

'Chang Liu? You've seen him too?' Lucy asked in astonishment.

'Chang Liu came through from the Forbidden City and stayed to help calm the children,' Amy Willet said. 'Oh, he has been a tower of strength, a charming old gentleman. You know that the Empress has fled, and the court is in disorder?'

'Tz'u Hsi has gone?' Lucy gaped at her.

'To Shensi, they say. Dressed like a peasant woman with her nails cut short. It's my personal opinion that she got off lightly, for she was a terrible woman though it may be unchristian of me to say so. The Boxers got into the Forbidden City, you know. There's talk of looting and other dreadful things.'

'The mandarin's servants—' Lucy began.

'All safe, my dear.' Amy Willet patted her hand. 'I have been teaching your Yang Fei some English customs and she is very quick to learn. It took our minds off worrying about you. Was that gunfire?'

She spoke with sudden alarm in her tired

face, as if she had not accustomed herself to the constant noise of warfare.

'It's thunder, I believe.' Lucy, too, frowned, her nerves jumping.

'A Peking storm is a frightening thing,' Amy Willet said.

'I ought to be with Chang Lee,' Lucy said, feeling fretful and childish.

'Nonsense, my dear.' Amy Willet pulled herself together with an effort and spoke briskly. 'Gentlemen never want their ladies with them when there's fighting to be done. Now that you're here you can help me roll these bandages. My! that *was* thunder! Oh, I do trust there won't be much damage done.'

Lucy, remembering the piles of crumbling stones and half-burnt, half-sodden wooden buildings they had passed on their way, thought the remark somewhat inappropriate, but then a flash of brilliant blue-white lit up the ward and the thunder crashed overhead.

'Here it comes,' Amy Willet said, with the grim satisfaction of a Cassandra whose worst prophecies have just been realised. 'You carry on with these and I will run over to make certain the children are under cover.'

She bustled off, and Lucy shook her head and applied herself as calmly as she could to her task. Later she would recall how tired she was, and how terrifying was the combination of gunfire and thunder, the mingling of fire-crackers with the lightning that had in it a cold and deadly beauty.

She rolled bandages, brewed urns of tea, ladled thin soup for soldiers whose nationalities were obscured by sweat and grime, greeted the mandarin when he came in with a group of small children clinging to the hem of his robe.

'My dear Lucy.' was all that he said, but she knew from the expression on his face that she was finally accepted as his daughter-in-law.

Darkness came and she was stumbling across the courtyard, too weary to avoid the deep puddles or to cower from the lightning. A tall figure, pistol tucked in his belt, came towards her, holding her tightly against him, pushing the hair back from her temples, kissing her upturned mouth, saying over and over.

'Lucy, I love you. I never meant to love a foreign woman but you came and everything I ever felt for Mei-Ling became a dream I'd hung on to for a long time. I love you, with your red hair and the funny way you screw up your nose when you're amused, and the quick temper that boils under your sweetness. If we both died at this moment we would have shared a little piece of immortality.'

'We're not going to die!' Something fierce and strong rose up in her, conquering her tiredness. 'We're going back to the House of the Willow and we have long lives ahead of us.'

'The willow itself is a symbol of immortality.' He raised his voice against the crashing of the storm, pulling her into the comparative shelter of the doorway. 'Remember that, if we don't meet again. The Boxers might—'

'Oh, don't say such daft things!' She drew away from him, her voice shrill with fright. 'Get back to your soldiers and make them defend the walls and stop—stop rattling on about immortality! Don't be so *Chinese!*'

'Lucy, you're a pearl!' He kissed her, his laughter defying the elements and was gone again into the driving rain.

The storm was at its height and the defenders on the parapets crouched low as the blue-white flashes of lightning eddied and skipped from wall to wall. A wind had come from nowhere, catching at her breath as she ventured into the open again. From one of the buildings she heard very faintly the sound of children singing. The indefatigable Mrs Willet had evidently organised some kind of singsong to chase away their fears. Soon the rebels might make their final assault, swarming over the walls with their glinting swords, but still the children sang.

Lucy groped her way to the sound and pushed open the door. The place had been a storeroom but now its half-empty sacks and bare shelves served as sleeping places. As she went in Amy Willet paused in her vigorous conducting and beckoned her over.

'The little ones will sleep through the greatest din,' she said, 'but the bigger ones need something to take their minds off things. This is a long night, my dear.'

'It's the night of the willow,' Lucy said slowly, lowering herself to the floor and taking a small boy on her lap. The child was half asleep, but he snuggled up in contentment, thumb in his mouth.

The hours passed and the singing grew

fainter and the storm itself slept under the curve of the moon.

Lucy woke from a half-sleep and struggled up, darts of agony cramping her limbs. In the greyness of dawn the faces of the sleeping children looked drained and waxen. She picked her way carefully between the huddled forms and came out into the splashed and littered courtyard. A small group of Chinese were engaged in trying to start a fire in one part of the square and several others were wandering about in a vague, bewildered manner.

'Lucy?' Stephen Just, looking very different from his usual debonair self, came towards her.

'What's happening? Why is it so quiet?' she asked.

'The Boxers have gone.' His voice was flat with weariness. 'They pulled out at the height of the storm. And a runner got through with news that our troops are on the way. They'll be here some time this morning. It's over. The rebellion is over, Lucy.'

'Have you seen Chang Lee?' she asked.

'He went through to the Forbidden City,' Stephen began.

Lucy whirled about and ran down the

narrow street to the little side gate. It stood open and unguarded now, and the streets beyond were washed with rain. Her eyes were still sleep blurred but the rising sun was warm on her head and her aching limbs were tingling into life.

Chang Lee stepped from the gateway of the house and she paused, gasping with relief.

He was alive, unhurt and, until that moment, she had not known how much she had feared that some twist of fate would snatch him from her. Against his shoulder he held the small Tong Su, wrapped in a blanket out of which his black head emerged like some dark flower.

'The boy was hiding in the pagoda,' he said. 'Mei-Ling and Chen Sula have gone. They went with the Boxers some time during the night and left the child behind. She took her dog.'

There was the pain of complete disillusionment in his face.

'The willow tree!' Lucy stared past him up to the small courtyard where the tree, stripped of leaves, its trunk charred and withered, bore mute witness to the fury of the storm.

'I could send Tong Su to the Mission,

if you'd prefer it,' he said.

Lucy turned her gaze from the blasted tree to the dark flower of the child and heard her own voice ring out, clear and joyous.

'Chang Lee, you must be clean daft! Where should a little boy be but in the house of his father!'

And she clasped her husband's hand as the sun finally broke through the clouds.

This Large Print Book for the Partially sighted, who cannot read normal print, is published under the auspices of

THE ULVERSCROFT FOUNDATION

THE ULVERSCROFT FOUNDATION

. . . we hope that you have enjoyed this Large Print Book. Please think for a moment about those people who have worse eyesight problems than you . . . and are unable to even read or enjoy Large Print, without great difficulty.

You can help them by sending a donation, large or small to:

The Ulverscroft Foundation,
1, The Green, Bradgate Road,
Anstey, Leicestershire, LE7 7FU,
England.

or request a copy of our brochure for more details.

The Foundation will use all your help to assist those people who are handicapped by various sight problems and need special attention.

Thank you very much for your help.